Copyright Page

The Draoidh's Gambit

© [2025] [Joseph L Wiess]

1

For permission requests, write to the publisher at:

[Golden Plains Press]

[JosephWiess@gmail.com]

ISBN: [979-8-9934166-3-2]

Cover Design: [Joseph L Wiess]

Edited by: [Joseph LWhite]

Printed in the United States of America

Dedication

To my family: love you all.

To My SubStack followers: Without you, this wouldn't be possible.

Contents

Mid Gearran

Year 300 post-founding

The traveler's cloak was dusted with snow, each flake melting into the worn wool before freezing again. The wind carried the dry scent of pine and woodsmoke , the breath of a hard land that had never truly yielded to the hands of men. Before him, the palisade walls of Eola rose out of the white plain like the bones of something ancient, blackened timbers half-buried in frost.

He paused beneath a leafless ash, the bark silvered with ice, and leaned his shield against his leg. The metal bore the faint mark of his unit almost lost beneath scratches and age, but here, in Eola, such symbols went unnoticed. These people worshipped in silence, if at all.

He unrolled his map, tracing his path with a gloved thumb.

"If I'm not lost, this should be Eola,"he muttered, rolling the parchment again before tucking it under his cloak.

He adjusted the strap of his shield, feeling its weight settle against his shoulder, and set out toward the town. The snow deepened around his boots, muffling the world to stillness. No birds called. Only the hiss of wind along the palisade broke the hush.

By noon, he reached the gates. Two carts stood waiting, oxen steaming in the cold, while a few bundled townsfolk went about their work with the quiet efficiency of people used to surviving on their own.

A guard raised a hand in greeting, or warning. His eyes narrowed as he looked the traveler over: the scarred armor, the easy poise of one accustomed to danger, the sword-hilt peeking from beneath the cloak.

"Welcome to Eola, stranger."

The traveler inclined his head slightly.

"Thank you," he grunted. "Where is the best inn in town?"

The guard blinked at the word *inn*; most here drank where they slept.

"The Black Swan is three blocks west and two blocks north. You can't miss it."

A nod of thanks, and the traveler passed beneath the gate.

Inside, Eola felt closer, narrower. Snow had been cleared into neat ridges along the bricked lanes, where water froze in shallow ruts.

The air was thick with smoke from hearth fires and the tang of iron from the blacksmith's yard. Somewhere a hammer rang; somewhere else, a child coughed.

The traveler stepped onto the wooden walk, pulling back his hood. The roofs leaned inward above him, their second stories jutting out like watchful faces. No temples crowned the streets, no shrines at the corners, only weathered charms nailed above doorframes: a braided cord, a carved stone, a sprig of withered heather. In Saorsa, even the smallest things could serve as prayers.

"Let's see, he said, three blocks west and two north."

He raked his fingers through brown hair and started on, the boards creaking beneath his steps.

Halfway down the street, a chill that had nothing to do with the weather ran through him. A whisper brushed the back of his thoughts.

[Stop.]

He froze, scanning the street. The sense of unseen presence stirred the small hairs on his neck.

[There, hiding in the alleyway.]

His gaze followed the goddess's intent until he found the shadow, a figure crouched where two buildings met, almost swallowed by the gloom.

"That ragamuffin?" he murmured.

[Keep an eye on her,] the voice breathed, faint as wind through pine.

"As you wish,"he answered quietly, leaning against the cold wall of a shop.

Across the street, the hidden figure stirred.

Feeling eyes upon her, she lifted her head, blue eyes wide and shining in the dim light. Her hair was a tangle of straw and frost.

When she saw the man standing opposite, her breath caught, and fear rippled through her like a shiver in thin glass.

"No, no, no," she whispered, shrinking deeper into the shadow.

No one in Eola spared her a glance. People in frontier towns learned not to see what troubled them.

[Shhh, little one. See that man over there?]

The wind carried the faintest warmth , a soundless voice she had long ago mistaken for madness.

[He's my Ridere. He will save you.]

"No, no, no. Nobody wants to save me; they want to hurt me."

Still, her eyes lingered. Perhaps it was the way he stood , calm, unafraid, as if he belonged to a world untouched by Eola's hardships.

Snow drifted between them, whispering against the boards.

After a few minutes, the traveler shook his head and resumed walking. The goddess's errands were never clear at the start, and he had learned to follow without question.

He had been on the road for five weeks. The thought of a fire, food, and a mug of ale felt almost holy.

Behind him, the woman glanced skyward.

"This is a bad idea," she murmured, but the sky gave no answer, only the distant rasp of a crow and the sigh of cold wind through the eaves.

She followed.

Chapter One

Of Heather and the Servant of Chains

The traveler paused at the threshold, squinting up at the sign that swung in the evening wind. The paint had faded to a ghost of its former brightness, an image of a stylized black swan, its wooden edges worn smooth by years of rain and laughter. A curl of warm light leaked from the cracks around the door, carrying with it the promise of fire and ale. He chuckled softly to himself before pushing the door open and stepping into the glow.

The scent of roasting meat and spilled beer struck him first, thick and familiar.

A dozen conversations blended into a single warm roar,the rise and fall of voices, the clatter of mugs, the low hum of a bard's lute from somewhere near the hearth.

He slipped through the front room, brushing past merchants in travel-stained coats and farmers too deep in their cups to notice. Beyond that was the common room, louder still, a swirl of heat and human scent that pressed close on all sides.

When the hairs on the back of his neck bristled, instinct urged him to turn. He stilled instead, jaw tightening. "She followed, didn't she?" he murmured under his breath.

The smugness from the goddess answered him without words, an amused warmth at the back of his mind, like the lingering taste of smoke. He sighed inwardly. Even though he might question his goddess, she'd never steered him wrong.

He willed the short hair at his nape to lie flat again, rolling his shoulders to ease the tension.

His eyes swept the room until they found an empty table near the center, close enough to see every corner, far enough from the hearth to keep his back cool. Moving toward it, he unhooked the shield from his shoulder and rested it on the opposite chair, the iron rim catching a flicker of firelight. His cloak came next, damp at the hem, draped over the back of his seat.

With a careworn sigh, he sat. The bench creaked beneath his weight. The noise and warmth swirled around him, comforting and alien all at once.

For a moment, he let himself breathe, feeling the press of the goddess's unseen attention soften, like a hand withdrawn from his shoulder. Then he folded his hands atop the table and waited for one of the serving girls to notice him.

Within minutes, he had a mug in his hand and a plate on the table and was enjoying a better-than-average meal. The stew's steam curled upward, mingling with the low haze of pipe smoke and the drifting scents of ale, sweat, and wood ash. Around him, laughter rose and fell in waves, punctuated by the occasional clatter of a chair or the bark of a barkeep.

The hum of life pressed close , a comfort and a cage alike.

Steeling herself, the woman paused outside the inn's door. The glow beneath the threshold spilled over her bare hands, trembling in the chill. Her breath fogged once, twice, and then she pushed forward. The hinges groaned softly as she slipped inside, head low, her cloak dragging in the rush of warm air that smelled of humanity and fire.

Quiet as a mouse, she hugged the walls, slipping through the front room where a merchant's laughter drowned the music of a lute. The common room beyond was busier still, men leaning over dice, a bard tuning his strings, a fire crackling under the watchful eyes of a mounted stag head.

And there he was, seated near the center of it all, a man in worn leather, eating as if he had all the time in the world.

Her heart thudded painfully. She retreated into a shadowed corner, pressing her back to the cool plaster. The goddess's whisper coiled through her mind, not words, not quite, but a pressure behind her ribs, insistent and merciful all at once. She murmured her response under her breath, eyes squeezed shut, bargaining for courage. When she opened them again, she caught sight of him lifting his cup, his profile lit by firelight and fatigue.

Gathering what resolve she had left, she slipped from the wall and began her approach. Every step was measured; the worn floorboards creaked beneath her boots like warning sighs.

The space between them felt impossibly long, filled with heat, noise, and her own fear. Her fingers curled tight in her skirts, ready to turn and flee if the goddess's promise failed her.

The man heard every furtive step she made. His hand stilled on his cup, but he didn't look up. Years of travel and worship had taught him how to listen, for footsteps, for lies, for gods. He inhaled quietly, catching the scent of damp wool and river mud, and felt the air around him tense as if the goddess herself were watching.

He held his breath as she sank to her knees beside him and whispered, "Please help me. She said you'd help me."

The words barely rose above the tavern's din, yet they cut through it cleanly.

He sipped his drink and kept the cup poised in one hand, eyes steady on the trembling figure at his feet. She repeated herself, the same plea, this time in the local Gaelic tongue, the cadence roughened by exhaustion.

She was on her knees, broken, battered, miserable looking, gazing up at him with concern in her blue eyes. A bruise darkened one cheek, and her hair, once fair, hung in limp tangles. The noise of the room seemed to recede, as if the air itself were holding its breath.

For a moment, he wondered if it was a trap. His gaze flicked around the tavern , a handful of patrons watching with mixed disgust and envy. Some women looked upon the kneeling stranger as though she were diseased, others as though they envied her desperation.

No, he thought. No one would stage this. This was real, painfully real.

He exhaled and dismissed the crowd from his thoughts, his attention returning to her bowed head. Her posture, her voice, her trembling , all spoke of ruin and faith entwined. And only one thing could mend either.

"What is it you want, woman?"

The common room had settled into a gentle lull. The fire had burned low, its embers breathing a red pulse through the haze of smoke. Outside, wind threaded through the shutters, sighing in counterpoint to the quiet murmur of patrons half lost to drink. At the center table, Balgair sat in the circle of warmth, his plate half-forgotten, the scent of roasted grain and honey still drifting from his cup.

She looked up at him through her tears and wild hair. "Help me, please, Maighstir. I can't do it anymore."

Her voice cracked the hush like a reed snapping underfoot. For a moment, even the fire seemed to draw a slow breath. He studied her—mud on her skirt, scratches across her hands, the faint shimmer of rain still clinging to her lashes. Beneath the dirt, she was a woman who had once known sunlight.

Her dress, though torn, carried the faded grace of freedom: fine cloth now dulled by travel, embroidery unraveling where it had caught on brambles. He imagined how others might have looked upon her in better days—with envy first, and then the cruelty that envy breeds.

"You can't do what anymore?" He lifted the mug, letting the honeyed scent of meadhon wash over him. The sweetness steadied his thoughts, a small ritual of patience. She whispered something that vanished into the noise of the room. "You'll have to speak louder, little one. I couldn't quite hear what you said."

She buried her face in her hands, shoulders trembling. Around them, a chair scraped, a laugh faltered, and then the tavern sounds drifted back like surf after a wave withdraws. When she raised her head again, her breath came in shallow gusts. "I can't live like this anymore." Her hand shook as she wiped her cheeks. "It hurts so much."

The lamplight trembled in the draft, laying shifting gold across her face.

Balgair felt the air change—an unseen current of grief thickening it, as though the goddess herself had leaned closer to listen. Understanding dawned; he said nothing at first, only watched the quiver of her lip and the weary rise of her chest. The anger he had mistaken for defiance was only sorrow wearing armor too heavy for her frame.

Even without touching her thoughts, he could read the exhaustion spilling from her. It concerned him deeply; he had not seen misery this pure in many seasons.

Somewhere beyond the walls, a bell tolled from the harbor, dull and distant—a reminder of the world still turning.

The council of Saor-Shelbs had made laws for souls like hers, laws meant to open doors rather than close them. All they needed was to find a man willing to listen, to bear witness, to help.

"Tell me of your pain, pretty one," he said, his voice a quiet command that steadied the trembling space between them.

"Please, don't tease me, Mhaighstir. I couldn't take it." She hugged herself tightly, the firelight catching on the torn edges of her sleeve. When he reasserted his command, the authority in it gentle but unyielding, she drew in a trembling breath and met his eyes for the first time.

"They told me I could do anything I wanted. They said that I could do anything a man could do. They said I could carry a weapon and go explore the world."

Her voice thinned to a whimper as her gaze drifted somewhere far beyond the tavern walls.

"This was not what you wanted, was it?" His question came softly, like a hand resting on a wound to still its bleeding. And slowly, word by word, she began to let the darkness spill out, the way smoke escapes from a shuttered flame.

"No," she whispered. "I wanted to stay at home, and I wanted to keep a house. I wanted to take care of children." She babbled like someone would hit her if she didn't get it out fast enough. "I want to cook and clean. I want to meet a strong man when he comes home at night and welcome him home with food, drink, and I... I want to dress like a courtesan" Her eyes widened in desire as she admitted what she wanted. "I want to dance for my Mhaighstir. I want to make him happy. I want him to take me and use me to satisfy his desires."

He watched the slow blush that marched across what he could see of her body as she gave voice to her deepest dreams. Before him, her eyes lost their distress and dilated as her body responded to her desires.

"What of the men here? Will none of them help you?" He glanced around the tavern again, judging the men gathered around the tables. With few exceptions, there weren't many he'd call real men. To a man, they looked as if they'd been domesticated.

He reached out with his prana and shook his head. There was not a single Mhaighstir among them, just the lost.

The woman at his feet shook her head. "No, Mhaighstir." She shivered as she felt his masculine energy wash over her. "Please, Maighstir, help me. I will do anything you ask."

"Anything?" He shook his head in disbelief. "We'll see about that," he promised, drawing a shiver of ecstasy and fear from the woman at his feet. Without breaking eye contact, he placed the mug on the table and gestured for her to come closer.

The fire had burned low, a red eye watching from the hearth. Shadows swayed across the tavern walls, moving in rhythm with the crackling of the logs. The smell of woodsmoke clung to the rafters, mingled with the faint sweetness of spilled meadhon and rain-soaked cloaks drying near the flames.

The noise of the room had thinned to a muted hum, as though even the air waited to see what would unfold.

She quickly crawled closer to him and sat back on her heels, straightening her body as she lifted her head. Her breath trembled; strands of hair caught the firelight like threads of copper as she brushed them over her shoulder.

For an instant, her movement sent ripples through the lamplight, and it seemed the whole room leaned inward. She nervously brushed her hair again and attempted to display herself to him.

"Not bad," he commented. "What do you want?"

A faint draft curled through the open door, stirring the candles until their flames bent toward the pair at the table.

The woman seemed to listen to a voice only she could hear. In a quiet voice, she whispered, "She's telling me that I should offer you my bond," the woman explained, shaking in fear.

The man shook his head. "You know she's not ready, milady." He whispered.

[What would you suggest?] The goddess inquired.

"Give her time to heal, then let her make her own choice," the man suggested.

The woman stared at him, her eyes wide. "You can hear her too?"

The man nodded. "I can." He leaned toward the woman. "Now, what is your name, young one?"

The murmuring around them dimmed again, as though the tavern itself held its breath.

The woman froze, wondering if he would like her name. She breathed slowly. "It is Heather, if it pleases you, Mhaighstir."

"It means 'Everblooming flower,' doesn't it?" he inquired. When she nodded, he leaned down and whispered, "It's a pleasure to meet you, Heather. I am Balgair."

The name hung between them like a spark caught in smoke. Hearing her name spoken with such tenderness brought tears to her eyes. "Does this mean you'll help me?"

"You could say that," he said as he stood up and placed the cup on the table.

The chair scraped softly across the wood. The woman watched as he rose to his full six-foot height, and she blushed slightly. She had expected him to be strong, as his prana suggested, but she hadn't expected this. Sitting, he was unremarkable. Standing, with his right hand resting on the hilt of his sword, he was every inch the guardian his goddess had shaped him to be.

The hearthlight caught in the black of his eyes as they traveled up and down her form—not with hunger, but with the calm appraisal of one charged to protect what was fragile. Around them, the tavern seemed distant, its laughter faded to an echo, the world narrowed to the space between them—one heartbeat of stillness before the goddess exhaled and the room came alive again.

The tavern had grown quieter as the evening crowd thinned. Smoke from the hearth coiled lazily toward the rafters, carrying the scent of oak and meat grease. Shadows stretched long over the floorboards, and somewhere a chair creaked under the weight of a dozing traveler.

"Now, for your first task," he walked toward the bar. "Follow me."

She rose quickly, her bare feet whispering against the wooden floor as she followed him through the dim glow of lanterns. The barkeep glanced up from polishing a cup, the reflected light glinting off his thinning hair.

"My good man, I would like two plates of food, a water bottle, and two cups. She will take them up to my room."

The barkeep's eyes flicked between them—the tall, black-eyed warrior and the pale woman hovering in his shadow.

"Aye," he said after a moment, voice low and worn. "He's in room four upstairs. Go to the kitchen and get him what he ordered."

When the woman hurried toward the swinging kitchen door, the smell of stew and onions followed her. The barkeep turned back to Balgair. "She's had a hard month, friend. I trust that you will...."

"Treat her as she needs to be treated," Balgair replied. "Our Lady of Chains has taken an interest in her and won't condone mistreatment of those under her blessings."

The barkeep's expression softened with understanding. The warrior turned toward the stairs, his boots echoing on the steps, then paused halfway up.

"If you can spare it, I would like to borrow a maidservant's dress for her until I can buy her new clothes tomorrow."

"I'll send Lucy up with a spare set," the barkeep said, already reaching beneath the counter.

Balgair nodded and climbed the remaining stairs, his hand resting on the worn rail. The air grew cooler as he reached the hallway, the noise below fading into the steady hiss of wind against the shutters. He hesitated at his door, the weight of uncertainty pressing briefly on his chest. A wry smile curved his lips.

What would Amelie say? Or Nell? He could almost hear their voices, Amelie's laughter, Nell's quiet disapproval softened by affection.

Inside, the small room carried the scent of oil and iron.

He set down his shield and began removing his chain mail, the links whispering like rain as he laid them aside. Through the window, the sky blazed with orange fire that melted slowly into violet. *Lady Ananke had never led me astray,* he thought, and yet doubt tugged at him like the wind against the shutters.

A soft voice pulled him from thought. "Maighstir, I have your dinner. My hands are full, and I can't get the door."

He grunted and crossed the room. The hinges groaned as he opened it. "Place the plates on the desk and come back here."

The woman obeyed, her footsteps careful against the wooden floor. The silverware rattled faintly as she set the plates down. "What is your will, Mo Maighstir?" Her voice was steady but small, her gaze fixed on the floorboards.

Alone with him, the silence pressed close; the smell of stew and damp cloth filled the space between them. She looked around, as if measuring the distance to the door.

"Heather," he said. Her head lifted at once. "The bath is through that door. I want you to go clean up, and when you are done, we will eat."

"Yes, Maighstir," she whispered. A pause, a shallow breath. "But I don't have anything to change into."

"We can't have that, can we?" he teased lightly, crossing to the bed where his pack rested. The leather creaked as he unbuckled it and searched inside. He drew out a folded bundle and tossed it toward her. "For now, put this on."

She caught it awkwardly, nearly dropping it. Unfolding the fabric, she found a silk shirt that shimmered faintly in the lamplight, falling to just above her knees.

Her eyes widened; she looked at him once, blinked, and fled toward the bath, the door closing softly behind her.

Balgair exhaled and rubbed the back of his neck. "What am I going to do with her?" he murmured, half to himself. The goddess's unseen laughter seemed to echo in the rustle of the curtains. "You would find that amusing, wouldn't you, My Lady?" he asked, shaking his head with a faint smile.

He moved to the window again, gazing out over the rooftops as twilight deepened. Every time he doubted her, Ananke proved herself through the women she guided to him—souls wounded beyond repair until divine intervention gave them new life. Amelie and Nell, once lost, now bound to him by shared grace and purpose.

A knock interrupted his thoughts—a soft, cautious sound. "Enter," he commanded, stretching out with his prana and brushing against the warm hum of feminine energy beyond the door.

The hinges creaked again, revealing a young woman in a tavern maid's outfit, holding a folded bundle. The firelight caught the sheen of sweat on her brow. "May I help you?" he asked, his gaze level and calm.

"Maighstir Brandyn sent me with something for Heather to wear."

He studied her face—something unreadable there, tension balanced between duty and envy. He didn't linger on it. "Come on in," he said, stepping aside.

The last embers of the fire glowed in the hearth, their light licking against the wooden walls.

Outside, rain whispered along the windowpanes, a steady hush that softened the edges of the room. The air was warm, heavy with the scent of soap, candle smoke, and meadhon lingering in the mug beside the desk. Balgair stood by the window, the dying sunset fading behind his reflection in the glass.

When she took a tentative step into the room, he turned. "Oh, the dress, right? She's through that door," he stated, gesturing toward the bathroom door. "She might need some help."

"Of course, Maighstir," she commented with a nod, then quietly padded to the door and softly pushed it open.

The light from the adjoining room spilled out in a pale wash across the floorboards, glinting against the links of his discarded mail.

"It's Lucy, sister. Maighstir sent me in to help you bathe and dress."

There was a softly spoken answer—just the shape of a voice, fragile and unsure—and Lucy slipped inside, closing the door behind her. The latch clicked softly, and Balgair exhaled, lowering himself into the chair near the window. He could hear muffled voices, the splash of water, the creak of floorboards. The rhythm of ordinary care—small, human, grounding.

A short while later, the tavern maid stepped back into the room. "Your Bond will be out in a bit. She's got a bad case of nerves."

There was that faint edge of anger in her voice. The air seemed to tighten. Before she could leave, he stopped her. "Enough of this, little one." The command was quiet but carried weight, like the snap of frost in the air.

He snapped his fingers and pointed to the floor at his feet. The gesture was habitual, ceremonial, a summoning rather than punishment.

The young woman hesitated, glare flaring in her eyes for the briefest instant, then her shoulders dropped.

She sank gracefully to her knees, the firelight painting her silhouette in bronze. Her palms rested flat on her thighs. The candle beside the bed flickered as though responding to his authority.

She looked down, refusing his gaze. "What is wrong?"

"Nothing," she snapped, then raised a hand to wipe away a tear. "I'm sorry," she muttered, "but your bond has gotten what I've wanted for the last five years."

Her words cracked something in the stillness, and for a moment the rain sounded louder. When she looked up, he gestured for her to continue.

"I've been working here for five years and desperately want to give my bond to Maighstir Brandyn." Her voice trembled. "He either doesn't notice, or he doesn't want me."

"Ah," he nodded, tone softening. "I understand." He shook his head slightly, shadows shifting across his face. "First of all, we aren't bonded, yet."

Lucy blinked in confusion, brows drawing together. "I don't understand. We saw you."

"You saw wrong. She's not ready to bond with anyone yet." He sighed, rubbing a hand over his face as though brushing off weariness. "Second, have you approached a servant of the chains and asked for their help?"

"No sir," she whispered. "There are no servants of the chains here. You are the first we've seen in several years."

"I'm not a chain-maker," he muttered under his breath.

The fire popped, and a faint, amused chime of laughter stirred the air around him. The candlelight rippled, as if a breeze passed through from nowhere.

He tilted his head slightly, his expression softening in reluctant amusement. "As you wish, my lady," he replied inwardly, voice barely audible. "When I come down later, I'll talk to your Maighstir Brandyn and see if he wants to bond you."

Balgair shook his head. "It seems my lady wants me to do her work."

The tavern maid's shoulders eased. She smiled gratefully—an unguarded, luminous thing—and rose to her feet, nearly running for the door. Her departure left a whisper of cool air behind her as the latch clicked shut.

Balgair stared at the closed door, the quiet settling around him again. The laughter of the goddess still echoed faintly in his thoughts. "What is wrong with the women in this town," he murmured, half in jest, half in weary affection.

Beyond the window, lightning flashed in the distance—silent, brief, like the blink of an unseen eye. He turned toward the sound of movement from the adjoining room as the bath door opened, and the faint scent of lavender drifted through the air. The fire stirred, brightening for just a heartbeat, and the chapter's last moment hung in that breath between stormlight and calm.

Chapter Two

The Calm Before the Storm

The room was hushed except for the faint hiss of the hearth fire, where the last of the wood crackled and collapsed into glowing embers. Shadows leaned long and soft against the walls, as if listening. A faint scent of lavender clung to the air , a trace of the soap from Heather's bath , mingling with the deeper notes of meadhon and old oak.

There was silence for a moment, and then Heather spoke. "Maighstir, here I am."

He turned. She stood framed in the bathroom doorway, the warm lamplight haloing her like sunrise after storm.

Nervously, she brushed her hands down the short thigh-length skirt that did little to cover her long legs. His gaze rose, not with hunger, but with quiet awe, past the lines of the skirt to the soft curve of the blouse that caught the firelight. Her heart-shaped face, framed by damp, dirty-blond hair, shone with a fragile kind of bravery. In her brown eyes, he saw both fear and the tremor of self-worth being reborn.

To say he was spellbound would be a lie. It was not enchantment that held him still, but reverence. The change in her was like the difference between night and dawn. With a small, approving nod, he gestured for her to approach.

There was a hint of a smile as she crossed the room, her bare feet whispering against the wooden floor.

The air around her felt different now, as though the goddess's unseen hand had lifted something heavy from her shoulders. She knelt at his feet, her voice soft but newly alive, and almost sang, "What do you think?"

"You're breathtaking." His lips curved into a smile. "Do you feel better?"

Caught off guard, she froze for a heartbeat, then answered timidly, "Yes, Maighstir, I do." She tilted her head, fingers combing through her hair, smoothing it from crown to tip. Her breath quivered as she spoke again. "It's most strange. I feel as if a great weight has lifted from me."

The flickering light dimmed as he moved toward the small table by the far wall. "Heather, come here."

She gazed at him, uncertain but sensing a test in his tone. Her eyes flicked from him to the table where the meal still waited, two plates, two cups, and the bottle of meadhon glinting gold in the lamplight. Understanding dawned, and she smiled faintly. Rising, she gathered the meal with grace, the practiced precision of someone once scorned for trying too hard. She carried each piece to the table, arranging them with care: his plate in the center, hers to the side, one cup before him, the other near her own.

Then, lifting his plate, the bottle, and a cup, she carried them carefully and sank to her knees once more. The floor creaked softly beneath her."Can this slave girl offer you food and drink, Maighstir?"

He blinked, caught between sympathy and unease. Of all the things he expected, this wasn't it. Something in him tightened, not anger, but sorrow. He briefly wondered if she was playing a role, or if the world had truly taught her to equate servitude with love.

Heather froze when she saw his expression. "Am I not a slave?"

He inwardly flinched, the question cutting through him like cold air. He had hoped for more time to lead her out of that darkness. "No, you aren't a slave." He hesitated, steadying his tone. "Nor are we bonded."

She looked lost for a moment, as though the floor itself had shifted. "If I'm not a slave, what am I?"

"You are a free woman," Balgair said softly, "under my protection."

The fire cracked, throwing gold across her features. She gave him a strange, almost haunted look. "Am I so unworthy that nobody wants me?"

"That's not it," Balgair replied, whispering a silent plea to Ananke that the fragile woman before him would not crumble beneath her own doubt. "Giving and accepting a life-bond requires trust." He knew it was half a lie; he'd accepted bonds under far worse storms. But he needed her to breathe before she bound herself to anyone. "I didn't think you were ready yet."

Heather sighed softly, tapping her fingers against her thighs, a nervous rhythm, half defiance, half thought. "Shouldn't that be my call?" she murmured. She lifted her eyes, voice trembling between pride and pleading. "What if I want to be your slave? Will you allow it?"

He nodded slowly, watching the tension leave her shoulders. She set the bottle and cup gently on the floor, then removed the thin square of cotan that covered the plate. Her movements were deliberate, reverent, almost liturgical. After a steadying breath, she lifted the plate with both hands and held it out, eyes lowered. "Your plate, Maighstir," she whispered.

He took it, placing it on the table with a gravity that made the act feel like a vow. She poured the meadhon with careful precision, filling his cup, then lifted it and held it up. "Your cup of Meadhon, Maighstir."

When his fingers brushed hers, a faint thrill passed between them, not desire, but recognition. She blushed, and the room seemed to brighten for an instant.

"You did well," he said, setting the cup down. Taking a piece of meat, he broke it in half and offered her one piece. "For you, my beautiful maiden."

She accepted it with both hands, tears pricking at the corners of her eyes as she tasted it , the first true offering she'd ever received without fear. A deep, quiet contentment softened her face.

When he gestured to the chair beside him, she rose and sat, movements small and precise. After a pause, she asked, "If I felt I was ready, would you accept my bond?"

Balgair leaned forward, studying her eyes , not as a man, but as a judge of spirits. *Can she be ready so soon?*

The air seemed to hum, a gentle vibration threading through his thoughts. *She might be,* whispered Ananke's voice, distant and clear.

He nodded slightly, then smiled at Heather. "If you feel you are ready, you can offer your bond and I'll accept it, then I'll give you mine."

The blond blushed again, lowering her gaze. "That voice I hear in my head, who is it?"

"Her name is Ananke," Balgair said, his tone softening to reverence. "She is our Lady of Chains."

"Chains?" Heather blinked, biting her lip. "Does that mean she's the goddess of slaves and bonds?"

He shook his head. "No. Ananke despises slavery. The bonds she facilitates are deeper and sharper than mere words and threats." He leaned forward and gently cupped her chin. "I would never hurt any of my bonds."

"Oh, I see," she murmured, her voice caught between awe and uncertainty. "You are bonded already?"

She sounded both disappointed and afraid. "May I ask a question?"

"You may," Balgair replied, reaching for a biscuit. He broke it, layered it with meat and cheese, and took a slow bite, the simplest gesture of mortal appetite, grounding the divine hush that lingered in the air.

The candlelight flickered low, spreading long golden shadows across the timbered walls. The inn was quiet now , the hum of voices below faded to a distant murmur beneath the steady whisper of rain on the eaves. The air smelled faintly of oak smoke and meadhon honey, warm and earthy, grounding the two souls within the small room.

Heather sat back on her heels, her breath a trembling thing as she considered which question might draw him out.

The goddess's silence pressed gently in the corners, like mist before dawn , unseen but felt. "When you stopped on the street and watched me, how did you know I was there?"

"Lady Ananke saw you first, then pointed you out to me." Balgair's voice held a calm certainty that filled the space like a steady flame. He studied her face, the quick flush rising in her cheeks, the nervous tightening of her hands , and felt the goddess's faint hum at the back of his thoughts.

"Aren't you going to eat?"

Caught by surprise, Heather blushed to her toes and mumbled, "Yes, Maighstir." Then, with him watching, she mimicked his motion and took a bite.

The bread was coarse but hearty, the cheese sharp. Her hunger betrayed her, and she coughed mid-bite, struggling to swallow.

"Are you okay?" he asked, half-rising, concern softening the edges of his otherwise battle-worn voice.

"I'm fine," she reassured him once she could breathe again. "I haven't eaten this much in a while." Outside, thunder rumbled faintly in the hills, distant, like the echo of some old god turning in sleep.

Balgair frowned, his gaze weighing her words with quiet disapproval. That she'd gone hungry offended something deep within him, a warrior's sense of justice, or perhaps the goddess's own indignation whispering through him. Heather caught the look and felt herself shrink inward, her heart tightening.

It should not have mattered , but now, for some reason, his opinion did.

"Was it by your choice?" he asked, his eyes scanning her with the precision of a healer, as if searching for unspoken wounds.
Blonde hair flew as she shook her head, "No, Maighstir. I was trying to avoid some people, and they like to hunt and torment me." Her words fell like pebbles into the silence that followed.

The hearth crackled, a single ember snapping. "If you want me to leave, I'll understand." Her voice was small, like something half-erased by wind.

"I don't think you'll be going anywhere," Balgair said quietly. There was iron beneath the gentleness now , the kind that forged oaths and broke tyrants.

For a heartbeat, the air around him shimmered, and Heather thought she saw the faintest glimmer of a chain wrought from light, circling him like a halo. He sounded as if he'd kill anyone who tried to take her away by force.

Heather brushed her arms as goosebumps rose along her skin. "I get to stay?" For the first time in many moons, hope stirred like spring water in her chest.

"Of course," Balgair nodded. "Milady would expect no less." His tone softened, and the faint glow in the air seemed to breathe away.

Heather sighed, relief leaving her shoulders slumped. The goddess's presence lingered faintly, unseen but listening. "Why does your goddess care what happens to me?"

Her voice carried all the bewilderment of a lost pilgrim asking the wind for direction.

"You'd have to ask her," Balgair said, shrugging. "I do know that Lady Ananke won't deceive you. She knows your circumstances and that changing your life will help you in some way. Who knows, you could be content, happy, maybe."

The flicker of candlelight caught the edge of his armor, and for an instant, the reflected light looked like stars shimmering on water.

Heather forgot to breathe. The words sank into her like sunlight on frost. She curled a strand of her hair around one trembling finger. "You said your name was Balgair?" When he nodded, she relaxed. "May I call you Maighstir Balgair?"

"Of course, you may." He poured
her a half-cup of the meadhon and passed
it to her. The golden liquid caught the
light, glowing like liquid amber. "Take
your time eating. We've got a bit of time."

"Until what, Maighstir Balgair?"
With a soft sigh, he leaned back. "Until I
do my Lady's work and make the young
tavern maiden a happy woman."

"Oh," Heather replied, her gaze
falling to the table. She watched his every
movement, uncertain which of them might
mean rejection. The bed in the corner
looked impossibly soft, and she thought ,
not for the first time , that she would trade
anything for peace.

"Shhh, calm down." His voice was
firm but kind. "If I need something, I'll tell
you." He reached across the table and
cupped her chin.

His hand was warm and steady. "If you worry about it all the time, you'll just wear yourself out, then what good would you be?" A candle guttered in the draft, its flame flaring high, as though affirming his words.

She exhaled, a tremor of breath escaping her lips.

Turning her face slightly, she brushed her cheek against his palm, a gesture of instinctive trust rather than submission. "I didn't know how you wanted me to behave."
She lifted her cup and shook it. "May I have more Meadhon, please, Maighstir?"

He nodded and poured her another half-cup. "Take it slow. I know it tastes sweet, but you'll get drunk if you aren't careful." He withdrew his hand, and she whimpered softly at the loss of warmth.

When he finished his meal, he pushed the plate away, leaning back with a low sigh. Heather, ever attentive, noticed that he'd eaten only half. Her own meal was barely touched. "Have you had enough, Maighstir?" she asked, reaching for the thin squares of cotan.

When he nodded, she quietly consolidated the food onto one plate, her movements deliberate, almost reverent. The hearthlight caught in her hair, giving it a soft amber sheen.

Balgair hid a yawn behind his hand and watched her with quiet fondness. The last echoes of Ananke's hum still shimmered in the air, a silver thread twining through the timbers of the room. The hearth's coals pulsed faintly, breathing warmth into the shadows.

Heather sat motionless for a time, her gaze turned inward, as though listening to something neither of them could see.

Then, softly, she rose. Her steps made no sound upon the boards. When her eyes fell upon his pack beside the bed, she hesitated, head tilted, waiting, perhaps, for the whisper of permission that hovered between them.

The the freedom Ananke granted through choice, not command—was already at work in her. She reached out and brushed her fingers across the weathered leather straps, tracing the scars of travel and toil like runes of a man's life.

The inn exhaled around them, its beams sighing with the weight of rain. Wind curled against the shutters, murmuring low through the eaves.

Somewhere within that sound came the ghost of laughter—soft, patient, and knowing.

The laughter of a goddess who wove destinies through tenderness rather than decree.

Heather knelt beside the pack. Her hair, a dull gold in the firelight, slipped forward like a veil as she unfastened the straps. Each motion carried the hesitance of one newly unchained, afraid that freedom might vanish if she moved too boldly. She reached within and drew out what lay hidden—first two bundles of folded clothes, which she placed reverently upon the bed, then a leather pouch that chimed faintly when lifted.

The sound of coin startled her; instinct drove her to press it between her thighs protectively, not as a thief, but as one who had learned too well that safety was never guaranteed.

From the depths of the pack, she lifted two daggers in polished sheaths, and two more leather sacks. These, she handled carefully before setting them back, as though she feared to disturb their slumber. When she was done, she lingered a moment, her breath shallow, eyes fixed on the belongings of a man who had shown her neither cruelty nor claim. Then, with deliberate care, she gathered the money pouch and tucked it between two layers of clothing, nestling it into the bedside drawer. It was an act of order, not possession—a small reclamation of peace.

When she turned back, her new maighstir was watching her through half-closed eyes, the faintest smile curling beneath his beard.

Balgair nodded at her. "You're learning."

The warmth in his voice drew something unspoken from her, a flicker of pride, still fragile but bright. She crossed the room and knelt again before him, the movement fluid now, less an act of submission and more a gesture of trust. When he crooked his finger, she leaned forward slightly, awaiting his word.

She looked as though she had more questions. When he nodded for her to speak, she asked softly, "Are you a priest?"

He confirmed her suspicion. "No, I'm not a Sagart of Ananke. Based on what you found in my pack, what do you think I do for a living?" He studied her expression as she weighed her answer.

"I think you are a soldier of some sort, Maighstir," she said, glancing toward the chain shirt and gambeson folded over the chair. "But you don't serve a church or a king."

When he raised a brow, she added, "I don't see a sigil or coat of arms."

The soldier grinned. "Correct. I am a mercenary and a member of the Black Hills Company."

She froze. "Do you have your own home?" The question came out too quickly, and she winced, fearing how it might sound.

Balgair laughed—a sound like gravel stirred by sunlight. "Yes, I have a saor-shealbh of my own. It's not large, but it's enough for me and my other two bonds."

The word *bonds* struck something deep within her. It rang like a bell beneath her ribs. She hadn't known anyone who shared a bond freely, without coercion or fear. "What are they like? Your bonds?"

His features softened, eyes far away. "Amelia is a firebrand and very outgoing. There are times she has no shame. Nell is a bit more reserved and doesn't brook stupidity at all." He looked at her again, a half-smile curving his lips. "You'll like them. If you stick around."

The words caught her breath. *If you stick around.* That was freedom disguised as invitation.

She had lived her life on borrowed ground; now, for the first time, she was being offered a place to stand. The thought sent a tremor through her chest. She looked away, blinking hard, and when the tears came, they surprised even her.

Balgair saw them and said gently, "It's okay, mo tè àlainn." He shifted in his chair and drew her up into his lap. "There's nothing that could make me kick you out."

For a moment, Heather stiffened, half-convinced he could see her shame written across her skin. But he didn't probe—he only held her. His warmth, the steady rhythm of his heart beneath her cheek, and the smell of leather and steel all blurred into something she hadn't known in years: safety.

"You'll like Amelia and Nell," he murmured. "It won't be long until you are part of our family."

The word *family* unfurled inside her like a sunrise breaking over snow. She sat rigid for a heartbeat longer, wrestling the ache of disbelief, then slowly yielded, resting her head on his shoulder.

Her sigh was a sound of surrender— not of will, but of weariness finally released.

Outside, the wind rose and bent around the inn, carrying with it the faint shimmer of divine laughter. The chains of Ananke did not bind here—they braided, linking souls by choice.

"Maighstir Balgair," she whispered, her voice steady now, "what did you mean when you said you would make Lucy happy?"

The lamps of *The Black Swan* burned low, casting amber light upon the walls like honey poured over stone. Beyond the windowpanes, the storm had gentled into a whisper, and the world outside shimmered with rain's memory. The air in the room still hummed faintly, not with sound, but with presence.

Lady Ananke lingered there, unseen yet palpable, like a thread of light coiled through shadow.

The mercenary closed his eyes, savoring the feel of the woman in his arms and enjoying the feel of her breath against his throat.

"It would seem that the lovely Tavern Maiden wants to be bound to the Tavern Master but doesn't know if he wants her." When she exhaled in surprise, he chuckled. "Lady Ananke finds it amusing but wants me to investigate and, if both wish it, bind them together."

Heather lifted her head and looked into his eyes. "Truly? I have seen the way Lucy looks at Maighstir Brandyn." She quirked a brow. "I should have guessed that she wanted his bond." When she saw the amused smile on his face, she blushed slightly. "What is it, Maighstir Balgair?"

"How easily you have called another man Maighstir." He commented.

She pursed her lips, her tongue flicking out to wet those lips. "Should I not?"

Balgair quirked a brow. "We aren't bonded, nor are you a slave. There's no need to call men masters."

Heather feared that she'd done something wrong and tried to explain. "Is it wrong to do something that feels right?" When he shrugged, she frowned, "You're no help. You're supposed to agree with me."

When he just gave her a disapproving look, she mumbled. "Why won't you agree with me?"

"Because you don't really don't want me to agree with you." He surmised. "Only you can speak for yourself."

Heather took a breath, then nodded to herself. "If I feel comfortable calling you Maighstir, then I should feel comfortable enough to call other men maighstir as well." She absently brushed her fingers through her hair. "If I do, then it is only right that I address them as such." She looked to him for confirmation, and when he nodded, she smiled, pleased. "When are we due downstairs, Maighstir?"

Balgair was amazed that she had so quickly accepted her new place, at least in her mind. "Probably right about now." He reluctantly let go of her and growled softly under his breath as she slid off his lap and stood before him. "We should also take our dirty dishware to the kitchen."

"Yes, Maighstir," she replied, reaching out for the dirty cups and the one plate they didn't need anymore. When ready, she looked over her shoulder and walked to the door. "Would maighstir please get the door?"

"Yes, of course," he replied as he opened the door for her. Then he led the way down the stairs and into the common room. While she disappeared into the kitchen.

The tavern was quieter now, voices subdued under the low growl of thunder in the distance. Lanterns swayed with the draft, casting gold upon the wet beams. Somewhere, far off, a temple bell tolled in the wind , its note carrying like a promise, or a warning.

With Heather safely busy in the kitchen, Balgair closed his eyes and conversationally whispered, "If it were any other than you, Milady, I would not intrude in another man's happiness."

At that, the presence that he associated with his goddess seemed to focus on him and he could feel Ananke's concern for him in the back of his mind. The faintest scent of jasmine and iron filled the air , the sign of her listening.

"I'm no chain maker, Mistress. I hope I don't mess this up too badly." He said as he opened his eyes and looked around.

The young lady from earlier was behind the bar, listening to the barkeep with avid attention. She looked softer now, the sharpness of her working day blunted by weariness and hope.

"Whatever I do, don't laugh, Milady."

After taking a cleansing breath, he casually made his way to the bar and leaned against it. "My thanks for your help, Lucy," he said, inclining his head to the tavern-maid.

"You're welcome, Maighstir," the brunette said as she watched him.

For a moment, Balgair wondered how to start his conversation. When his eyes fell on the great axe hanging behind the bar, he took a minute to appraise the weapon. Its edge gleamed faintly, as though remembering old wars. "I've come across very few men who can wield one of those easily."

The Tavern Master gave Balgair the once over and grunted. "You might be able to."

"Who me?" Balgair shook his head. "I like my sword and shield too much to want to pick up one those."

The barkeep raised one brow. "I saw you when you came in." He leaned down. "By the way, did you see the sign hanging outside, Captain?"

Balgair leaned back, trying to remember if he had left his shield uncovered. The silence stretched, not tense, but heavy with understanding.

It was apparent that he must have, because the man introduced himself. "Sergeant Brandyn de Rute." He gestured over his shoulder to the shield hanging on the wall.

Balgair, remembering the sign hanging outside, chuckled. "I was wondering why it was called The Black Swan. I'm Balgair Moeldr," he said, extending his hand.

Brandyn gave Balgair another long look. "You present the appearance of a man under orders."

Balgair grinned tiredly. "Aren't we all? Though I'm not sure what I have to discuss will sit well with you."

The big man arched a brow. "You'll never know if you don't talk about it." He commented, bringing his mug to his lips to take a drink.

"You're right," the mercenary admitted. "Have you ever considered the advantages of having a bhanna?"

Brandyn coughed up a bit of the ale he had swallowed. "Of all the things I expected you say, that wasn't it." He admitted. After carefully placing the mug on the bar, he wiped his mouth. "You don't look like any chain-maker I've ever seen."

"I'm not a chain maker," Balgair reflexively said. "I'm just a follower of Our Lady."

Brandyn sniffed. "That has a ring of truth to it, because you don't look like any priest I've ever seen." When Balgair managed to shrug, the barkeep rolled his eyes. "I feel like I'm being set up for an ambush, but yes, I have occasionally wondered what kind of woman would bond with an ex-soldier."

He glanced over at Lucy, noticing the blush crawling down her neck. "Might you know of such a woman?"

Before Balgair could answer, Heather appeared at his side and sank to her knees. "I'm done, Maighstir."

Balgair absently thanked her and turned to continue his conversation with Brandyn. That was, until he heard heavy footsteps behind him and a menacing voice said, "We've been looking for you, Heather. Imagine finding you here, dressed like a maid."

The warmth of the tavern seemed to collapse inward. The laughter at the back tables faltered. Rain hissed against the shutters like whispering serpents. Ananke's presence vanished, not in abandonment, but in warning.

Balgair's hand slid toward his sword, and the lamplight flickered like a heartbeat before battle.

Chapter Three

The Black Swan in the Street

The common room's laughter died like a candle snuffed by wind. Hearth smoke hung thick and low, curling through beams of amber light as the door slammed open to let in the rain. The warmth seemed to draw back into the stone itself. Heather was on the floor, her forehead pressed to the cold flagstones, trembling so hard the rushes shifted beneath her knees. Every muscle in her body screamed submission, but the fear in her eyes told a different story , one of survival.

When Balgair turned, he didn't need to ask why. The man behind her, tall as a temple door and twice as broad, filled the tavern's entryway.

His bald head gleamed in the firelight; his eyes were gray pits that swallowed the room's glow. His voice, when it came, was a weapon.

"Nothing to say, woman?" he sneered, his words thick with ale and cruelty. He nudged her side with the tip of his boot. "I'm talking to you, bitch."

The patrons froze. The hearth crackled nervously, its fire whispering against the silence. Without thought, Balgair stepped between them , a single, fluid movement born of habit more than decision.

"I'm just starting," the brute smirked, circling to jab at Heather again. "If this is what you wanted to be, I could have put a collar around your neck."

The mercenary's expression darkened, and though his tone stayed even, his voice carried like a drawn blade. "I don't think she wants to be anywhere around you. Why don't you take the hint and leave her alone?"

His words struck the air like thunder beneath velvet , no louder than before, but full of weight. The brute laughed, an ugly, barking sound that didn't quite hide his unease.

"Har, you're funny, stranger." He stepped in and drove his foot toward Heather again, this time harder. The sound of her body hitting the floorboards cracked something open in Balgair.

"You don't have the balls to—"

He never finished. Balgair's fist came up in a flash, the strike fast and merciless. Bone met bone with a sharp report, and the brute reeled backward, blood welling from his split lip.

"What are you made out of, stone?" Balgair muttered, shaking out his fingers. The old rhythm of violence hummed beneath his skin, familiar and steady as prayer.

Brandyn's voice broke the silence, deep and certain. "Brutus, you've had enough. It's time to leave." He hefted the axe from behind the bar, the polished edge catching the firelight. "No sane woman will have anything to do with you, not after what happened to the last three."

The brute spat blood onto the floor. "I nach do rinn nothing, and you na dean have proof that I did." His grin returned, thin and mean. "And you, Boyo," he said, eyes narrowing at Balgair, "you just signed your death note."

"Hold on," Balgair said, glancing toward the barkeep. "Last three? What happened?"

Brandyn's disgust was plain. "This person collared three different women, and all three died within weeks."

The words sank into the floor like spilled oil, and every soul in the tavern seemed to hold its breath. Balgair looked down to find Heather watching him through her hair , fear and fragile hope caught in the same trembling gaze.

"Heather is not going anywhere with you," he said, his tone low but unyielding.

"Who's to stop me?" the brute sneered, a tooth gone from his grin. "You?"

Balgair's reply came calm and sure. "You'll drag her out of here over my dead body."

"That can be arranged," Brutus spat, his voice slurred with rage. He bent low, close enough for Heather to smell the rot of his breath. "After I've killed this un, I'm gunna drag ya out of here and make ya scream like the slut you are."

Heather whimpered, a small, broken sound that somehow cut through the room more sharply than the earlier violence.

"Let's go, boyo," Brutus growled. "I've got things to do today."

Balgair's eyes hardened, the shadows deepening around him as though the fire itself deferred to his will. "Let's take this outside." His voice carried like iron on frost. "I'll be out in five minutes. That should give a coward like you enough time to set up your little ambush."

Brutus spat again and stomped out, his boots thundering against the porch boards until the sound was lost in the rain.

For a long moment, no one moved. Then, slowly, the tavern began to breathe again. The hearth crackled louder, the storm's howl slipping through the open door like the whisper of unseen gods , and Balgair stood there in the center of it all, his jaw set, his shadow long and dark across the floor.

The tavern still thrummed faintly with the echo of Brutus's departure, a vibration in the floorboards, like the aftershock of an earthquake waiting to finish what it started. The scent of smoke and spilled ale hung low in the air, mingled with the faint metallic tang of fear. Outside, the muted roll of thunder over the moors whispered warning through the eaves.

Balgair exhaled, the tension leaving him in a visible shiver. "Well, well, mo te alainne, you do know how to pick them." His voice carried the trace of wry affection, the kind that masked old weariness. He reached down to help Heather rise. The firelight caught the tremor in her hands before his steadied them.

"Are you okay?" he asked, holding her at arm's length, his eyes scanning her for hurt like a battlefield physician assessing the fallen. "I think you'll live."

Heather sagged against him, the relief in her breath soft and human. When she leaned close, he returned the contact, a protective embrace that, for a heartbeat, stilled the restless murmur of the room. "Go upstairs and get my shield and chain shirt. Bring them back down here." His words were gentle command, the voice of habit and care entwined. He smiled faintly as she turned, nearly running for the stairs. "Slow it down, girl. I've got five minutes."

The boards creaked as she ascended. For a moment, the tavern seemed to breathe again, fire snapping, rain beginning to patter softly against the shutters.

The smell of wet earth seeped in, mingling with smoke and stew, the world grounding itself after violence.

Balgair turned to the barkeep, his tone shifting from human warmth to the iron calm of a commander. "If this brute has killed three women, why hasn't he been arrested?"

Brandyn's jaw tightened as he set the axe on the bar, the blade catching the glow of the fire. "Our sheriff died a while back, and none of his men have been brave enough to try to arrest him." He nodded toward Balgair. "If the boss trusted you enough to make you a Captain, maybe you can beat him." The barkeep leaned against the counter, the weight of memory behind his eyes. "And when you're done, I'll discuss Lucy's well-being with you."

"When this is over, we'll have a long talk about her and how you know my boss," Balgair said. His tone was flat, almost ritual.

Inwardly, he was already counting heartbeats , five minutes, no more.

Above them came the crash of Iron against stone and Heather's startled cry. "Help!"

Balgair was already moving when Brandyn barked, "Lucy, give her a hand!"

The girl dropped her cloth and ran up the stairs. Within minutes both women reappeared, stumbling, burdened by iron and steel. Lucy fought to control a kite shield almost larger than herself, while Heather struggled beneath the drape of chainmail that swallowed her small frame.

"How do you carry this, Maighstir?" she gasped, half-laughing through her effort. "This is heavy."

The other woman, cheeks flushed, looked at Balgair as though seeing him for the first time. "I didn't realize how strong you were," she whispered, kneeling and bracing the shield against her chest.

Brandyn chuckled and leaned forward, his hands thick as knots of rope. He lifted the shield in one easy motion, setting it on the bar. "I've got it, girl."

"I don't carry it wrapped around me," Balgair said, his voice low and amused. He leaned down carefully unwrapping the chain from Heather's body. His gauntlet brushed her by accident, the soft underside of her breast, and the startled gasp that followed was too human to ignore. A blush rose like dawnlight up her throat, and she looked away.

"I wear it like this," he continued, his tone matter-of-fact, the motion fluid and practiced. The chainmail slid over his shoulders with the weight of memory, each ring a whisper of past battles and oaths sworn. "The weight of the chain is distributed across my body, starting with the shoulders and around my hips," he explained, fastening his sword belt back over the armor with a soft clink.

For a moment, he softened again. He reached down, fingers brushing her cheek, a soldier's blessing. She turned her head and kissed his palm, eyes bright beneath the tavern's dim light.

Behind the counter, Brandyn muttered almost reverently, "I didn't know that you were An Eala Dhubh."

The tavern seemed to still at the name. The Black Swan, soldier of the great council, men who went where others dared not go. The hearth's flames guttered once, as though acknowledging the invocation.

The barkeep lifted the shield and handed it over. Balgair raised a brow. "You didn't pay much attention to the sign outside, did you?"

When the soldier shook his head, Brandyn pointed behind him. There, carved into oak and burnished by smoke, was the tavern's crest: a black swan with three pale bars beneath its wings, the mark of old campaigns and shared blood.

"Interesting," Balgair murmured, tracing the familiar sigil. "When did you serve?"

"About five years ago," Brandyn replied. He wiped the face of the shield, the rag catching the dull gleam of iron. "How is Maighstir Darkblade doing?"

"He should be back from tri aibhnichean by now," Balgair said. His tone was wistful, respect wrapped in memory. "They were on their way to hunt an Orcan war band."

"That's interesting," Brandyn mused. "I figured you worked for General Oberon instead of Rhyslin." He gave a conspiratorial grin. "Is that temperamental black-haired woman still begging for his bond?"

"Rowena? Yes, she's still there and still begging for that bond." He sighed softly. "Speaking of changes, it's just about time."

He turned back to Heather. Her eyes followed his every motion, the way one might watch a torchbearer walking into a storm.

"Do me a favor and wait here," he said quietly. "I should be back soon."

Heather swallowed hard. For a moment she thought he was memorizing her face, the line of her jaw, the tremor of her lips. She offered him a shy, trembling smile. "Be careful, Maighstir," she whispered, cheeks coloring. "I don't want you to die because of me."

Balgair's own smile was weary but warm. "I doubt it will come to that." He chuckled. "Besides, Nell would pay someone to bring me back, and then Amelia would geld me."

His humor softened the heaviness of the moment. "I have no intention of allowing that man to beat me."

He hefted the shield, feeling the sigil's weight as though his goddess herself had laid a hand upon it.

"Can you watch over her until I get back?" he asked.

Brandyn nodded. The oath hung unspoken in the air, iron between men of the same order.

The Black Swan took a long breath, tasting the tavern's smoke and rain, the mingled scent of hearth and storm. Then he turned toward the door, stepping into the gathering dusk.

The hinges creaked softly behind him, and as the door closed, the last light from the fire caught the swan etched on his shield, a dark wing poised between shadow and flame.

The street lay still beneath a shroud of gray light, the snow having drawn back to the hills.

Mist coiled in the gutters like breath from the sleeping earth, and from somewhere high above, the faint hum of Lady Ananke rippled through the air, not a sound, but a tremor in the soul, like the string of a harp plucked by unseen fingers.

Balgair stepped out into that silence, the iron scent of rain and blood already whispering through his memory. He paused, scanning the lane.

The brute stood bold and centered, his spiked club swinging idly, while a shadow lingered at the edge of a nearby building, a crossbowman half-swallowed by the fog.

Balgair angled his shield toward the hidden man, the swan sigil catching the weak sunlight like a coal ready to flare.

"Seall, there's the funny one," the brute snickered as Balgair came forward. His voice was a sneer that stained the air. "Well, well, this should be fun. I've never killed a black swan before."

"I wouldn't count your wyvern eggs just yet," Balgair said, his tone measured, a soldier's calm sharpened to a razor. He strode forward with the gait of one who had long since made peace with death. "I'd ask if this were a fair fight, except I've already found your hidden assassin."

He proved his point with a flick of motion, the dagger spun and sang through the air, thudding into the timber near the crossbowman's face. Wood splintered, and the shadow jerked backward with a curse, melting deeper into the alley.

"It looks like you missed," the brute jeered, lips curling.

"If I had been aiming to kill, he'd already be dead," Balgair replied, hand resting on the hilt of his sword. His eyes narrowed slightly. He was already counting heartbeats, the rhythm of the coming death.

Brutus grinned, showing cracked teeth. "Are there any last words you want me to pass along to whichever woman is unlucky enough to be cleaning your slop?"

Balgair stopped four feet away, mist curling between them like ghostly breath. "Let's go, you degenerate. I've got better things to do than play with you all day."

"Do you?" Brutus hefted his club and advanced, his boots thudding in the wet dirt. "Fine, let's get this over with. The sooner I kill you, the sooner I can enjoy the body of that little whore."

"You wouldn't know where to stick your dick," Balgair shot back, his tone a blade of contempt. "Knowing you, you hit the wrong damned hole."

Rage twisted Brutus' face, but before he could react, Balgair flexed his knees and drove forward, sword flashing in a clean, economical thrust.

Steel met leather and bone, the strike glanced off as Brutus barely managed to parry with his club. Sparks danced between them, dying quick as flies in the rain.

From the alley came the soft, betraying *twang* of a crossbow.

Balgair moved before he thought, the shield lifted, divine instinct guiding the motion. The bolt struck the rim and spun away, humming into the dust.

He took another step forward, slashing diagonally, the blade singing a low note of fury as it carved from waist to shoulder, tearing through the man's armor.

"Damn you, boyo. Now I'm going to kill you," Brutus spat, tracing the cut as though it were merely an inconvenience. "I've heard that sluts love scars. Maybe yours will love mine."

Balgair's lips curved, though his eyes had gone cold. The light of the dying sun flared along his shield's polished edge, a sudden, searing beam that struck the alley. The assassin cursed and ducked back, blinded.

The Black Swan smiled faintly.

"There's no shame in withdrawing in the face of a superior swordsman," he murmured.

"Stay still, ya fooker!" Brutus roared, swinging the club in a wide, heavy arc, all muscle, no grace.

What followed was less a duel than a dance, the *Dance of the Dead*, as the old mercenaries called it.

Where Brutus lunged like a beast, Balgair flowed, shield, sword, and breath all one continuous rhythm.

The edge of his blade whispered across the brute's knee, then darted upward like a striking serpent toward his shoulder. Blood darkened the leather.

"That's what you get for not having stamina," Balgair taunted, circling lightly. "Then again, you probably fight like you make love. Wham, bam, thank you, ma'am."

The words landed like a slap, driving Brutus into a fury that robbed him of thought. His club came down in a killing blow.

Balgair stepped forward and half-turned, catching the strike on his shield, the impact shuddering up his arm.

Before the brute recovered, the flat of Balgair's sword cracked across his right elbow.

Bone splintered. The scream was short, ragged, wet.

"Yer gonna pay for that, boyo," Brutus growled, switching the club to his left hand, trying to raise it again.

"I wonder," Balgair said mildly, dipping low and preparing his next block, "do you practice using that cudgel with your offhand?"

The next swing came slower, clumsier. Balgair caught it with his shield, pivoted, and hooked his boot behind the brut's knee.

"I guess not," he murmured as he wrenched back. The bigger man crashed down, landing on his shattered arm with a roar that sent pigeons scattering from the rooftops.

Then came the end.

With the patience of a craftsman finishing his work, Balgair drove the shield into Brutus' other arm. The snap of bone echoed down the narrow street.

"Now," he said conversationally, voice almost kind, "what was that you said you were going to do to Heather?"

He didn't wait for an answer. The sword swept low, cutting the back of Brutus' leg, muscle parting cleanly. The brute toppled again, shrieking.

"Oh, that's right," Balgair said, stepping behind him, "you were going to make her scream like the slut she is." His boot lashed out, a single, punishing kick that shattered the man's hip and sent him sprawling.

"Mercy, please," the brute begged, chest heaving.

Balgair drew back his sword. His face was unreadable, not rage, not pity. Only purpose.

"Why?" he asked softly. "You would have shown no mercy to either her or me."

The sound of another *twang* cut through the silence, and the arrow struck home, not in Balgair, but in Brutus.

The ruffian gasped, a feathered bolt blossoming from his ribs.

"You need to learn to aim better," Balgair called toward the alley, his tone dry. "You hit your own man."

He advanced, closing the space between him and the would-be killer. The assassin stumbled backward, and from the shadows, two ragged shapes emerged. The homeless men, watchers of fate's low tide, moved with brutal efficiency.

A kick to the groin. A slice of rusted steel. The crossbow clattered to the cobbles.

Balgair smiled grimly. "Just goes to show, you should always watch your back."

When he turned again, Brutus was still breathing, though shallowly. Blood spread like a dark tide beneath him.

"Now, you were begging for mercy, right?" Balgair said as he approached.

"You can't kill me. You're a soldier. You have rules."

"I'm a mercenary," Balgair replied, kneeling. The sun caught in his hair like flame on bronze. "The only rule I have is not to hurt the innocent." He placed the tip of his sword over the man's chest. "You, my friend, are no innocent."

He bowed his head slightly, voice lowering to the cadence of a prayer. "May Nan Diathan have mercy on your soul."

The sword came down, clean, final.

The air shivered. The mist rose in a sigh, curling upward like incense.

Balgair stood, wiping the blade on the dead man's tunic. "Nobody is going to miss you," he whispered, sliding the sword home.

The swan upon his shield caught the waning light, black upon silver, poised between grace and death.

And so the Lady's justice was done.

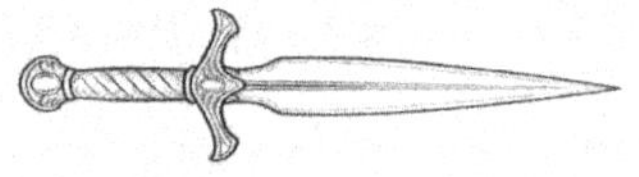

The rain had slowed to a mist, leaving the street slick and silver under the lanterns. The puddles glowed faintly, each holding a reflection of the heavens above, fractured stars trembling in muddy water. Balgair stood for a moment beside the bodies cooling on the cobblestones, his breath visible in the damp air. The tang of iron and the sharpness of fear still clung to the stones, though the goddess's hum, low and steady, had begun to ease.

He turned toward the two homeless men crouched by the assassin's corpse. One was old and thin as wire, the other broad-shouldered but hollow-eyed. They moved with the nervous speed of men used to being chased away.

"Did he have anything of value?"

The older man straightened, his face wary under the streetlight. "He had some coin, his clothes, and weapons." He eyed the mercenary as though weighing his soul. "You gonna take it away from us?"

Balgair shook his head, a tired smile touching his mouth. "No, in fact, I was going to offer you some more coin."

The younger man snorted. "Right, and I'm Father Yule." When the mercenary laughed, the man scowled. "It weren't meant to be funny."

A faint breeze wound between the buildings like a sigh, stirring the edges of Balgair's cloak. Somewhere in the darkness, a church bell tolled, not for the dead, but to mark their passing on to whatever justice awaited them.

"I know," he said lightly, "If you can take off both bodies, you can have what they've got on them, plus I'll give you a handful of coins to clean the mess up."

The men exchanged glances. Rain dripped from the awning above, beating a soft rhythm against the cobbles. "How much coin?" asked the first.

"Enough to get you off the street for a week," Balgair offered. "If you want it."

The second man whispered something to the first, the sound lost beneath the patter of water. After a beat, he nodded. "You've got a deal, sir. We'll drag the bodies to the undertaker. We get what's on them, and you'll give us a handful of coins on top of that."

Balgair nodded. "Exactly." From behind his belt, he drew a small leather pouch and tossed it to the closer man. The pouch landed with a heavy jingle, and the man caught it, blinking in disbelief at its weight.

"Thank ye, sir."

"No, thank you, Father Yule," Balgair replied, grinning as the goddess's laughter, quiet and crystalline, rippled through the fog.

The two men burst into rough laughter of their own, startling a stray dog that had been watching from the shadows.

"Jang, sir," said the first, thumbing toward his companion, "and me friend is Fred. If you need us for any other dirty work, just call."

"I'll do that," the mercenary said. The fog thickened around him, curling in ghostly shapes as he turned toward the inn. The scent of wet stone and iron gave way to the warmer aromas of stew and smoke as he crossed the threshold.

Balgair pulled out a piece of cloth and wiped his forehead as he stepped onto the porch and approached the door. "That could have been worse," he muttered, his voice lost in the hiss of the rain. He pushed the door open and was met by the soft hum of life, laughter, conversation, the crackle of fire.

The first thing that greeted him was the smell of cooking meat stew. As he walked past the bar, Brandyn stopped him with a wave.

"How did it go?" He took a good long look at the Captain.

"About the way it usually goes when an untrained fighter picks on a soldier," Balgair said with a shrug. "I got rid of the big guy and a pair of bums killed the assassin."

"What did you do with the bodies?" The barkeep inquired curiously.

"I got the bums to cart them off. Told them they could have what's on the bodies, plus I gave them a handful of coins for their trouble." He glanced around, looking for Heather. "Where did my charge go?"

Brandyn held his hands up. "She couldn't bear the thought of you being hurt, so she ran up to your room to hide."

"At least I know where to find her," Balgair commented as he headed upstairs.

"I'm going to clean up and then we'll be back for some of that stew."

The barkeep grinned, "Good, I'll save you some." He inclined his head. "I haven't forgotten that you wanted to talk about Lucy." He teased, bringing a blush to the maiden's face as she heard him.

As the tavern door swung shut behind him, the air seemed to shimmer faintly, Ananke's unseen gaze lingering a heartbeat longer before fading into silence. Outside, the snow covered the blood on the cobblestones.

Balgair laughed quietly to himself as he ascended the stairs, the wood creaking beneath his boots like an old friend sighing with relief. The sounds of the common room faded behind him, the clatter of dishes, the low hum of Brandyn's voice, replaced by the muted hush of the upper floor. A stray breeze from a cracked window carried with it the faint scent of rain and iron, cleansing and sharp, as if the world itself sought to wash away the blood he'd shed.

He paused at his door and knocked softly. "I'm back, mo te alainne."

When he opened the door, the room was dim save for the light of a single oil lamp flickering on the table. Heather knelt at the foot of the bed, the lamplight gilding her hair so it seemed spun from pale gold. Her face lifted at his voice, joy breaking over her like dawn after storm.

"Balgair, oh Balgair," she cried, rising half to her feet before he stopped her. When she froze, crestfallen, he offered a small, tired smile.

"Hey, it's okay," he murmured, reaching back to tug at the chain shirt that clung to him like a second, blood-slick skin. "I've got his blood all over me. I didn't think you'd want it on you."

The metallic tang of dried blood filled the air as Heather hurried to his side, fingers trembling as she helped lift the chain mail over his head. Her touch was gentle but sure, and the links whispered like falling rain.

"I was concerned that you might get hurt," she said, voice small but steady. She sniffed, holding a handful of mail. "How do you clean this?"

"Just concerned?" he teased, a ghost of humor softening the fatigue in his eyes. "Is that why you were crying at the end of the bed?"

Heather's eyes widened, catching the lamplight like glass. "Well, if anything had happened to you, Brutus would have pulled me out of here, kicking and screaming."

Balgair arched a brow, his smirk wry. "Would you have now? To get the blood off the armor, we'll dunk it in water, along with my shirt and pants." He unfastened his shirt and let it fall to the floor.

Heather gasped softly. The lamplight revealed a map of scars across his back , pale ridges and darker lines, the language of every battle he'd survived. "Do they hurt?" she whispered, tracing one with a fingertip, reverent as a priestess reading an inscription.

Balgair shook his head, voice low. "No, I've almost forgotten about them." He reached for his belt, smirking again. "I'm about to get out of these. If you want to protect your virtuous reputation, I'd move."

A rueful chuckle escaped her. "My virtuous reputation was destroyed after Brutus killed my parents and raped me." Her voice trembled, not from shame but from release, like a wound finally breathing. Before he could respond, she slipped her arms around him, resting her cheek against his back. For a heartbeat, the air stilled, as though the goddess herself held her breath.

He let her cling to him, feeling her trembling quiet under his steadiness.

The flickering lamplight dimmed and then brightened, a subtle pulse that felt almost alive. After a time, he gently untangled himself. "Could you get me a change of clothes?"

"Of course," she murmured, moving toward the small chest beside the bed. The soft sound of cloth rustling was oddly comforting. "Are we going downstairs?"

Balgair nodded. "Brandyn is saving us some stew. I thought you might be hungry."

Heather smiled faintly, her voice warm again. "You're such a gentleman. Always thinking of us poor women." She waited as he dressed and pulled on his boots. The scent of steel and sweat gave way to the softer aromas of stew drifting up through the floorboards. "I'm ready when you are."

When they descended to the common room, the air was thick with the rich fragrance of simmering broth and roasted herbs. Firelight from the hearth flickered across Brandyn's scarred face as he gestured them to a newly cleared table.

"Now where were we?" Brandyn asked, pushing a steaming bowl toward Balgair.

The mercenary accepted it with a nod. "This is very good," he said after a spoonful. "I believe we were talking about bhanna."

"Thank you," Brandyn said, hooking a thumb over his shoulder. "Though the thanks should go to Lucy. She fixed the stew."

"I'm glad you like it," Lucy said, smiling shyly as she clung to Brandyn's arm.

Brandyn's expression softened, but his voice was gruff. "Why should I bond with her when I can just take her and make her mine?"

Lucy's eyes flashed, spoon raised like a tiny weapon. "Why you! What makes you think you can just take me?"

"Five years of you mooning after me," he countered, leaning down with a teasing glint. "Do you mean to tell me that if I were to carry you upstairs and ravish you, you'd fight me?"

"No," Lucy squeaked, pressing her face against his shoulder. "You know I wouldn't." Then, quieter: "You're mean. You're supposed to want to join our hearts together and tell me that you'll keep me forever."

When Brandyn didn't answer, she looked toward Heather, who nodded in solidarity. "See, she agrees with me."

Brandyn exhaled, running a hand through his hair before meeting Balgair's calm gaze. "By Nan Diathan, woman. You must know that I care about you."

When Lucy nodded timidly, he sighed. "Balgair, can you help us with the bonding ceremony?"

Balgair winced as a ripple of divine laughter filled his chest. The air around him shimmered faintly, a pressure, a warmth, as though invisible chains of light coiled and danced at the edge of sight. "Yes, I can," he whispered, silently begging Ananke to still her joy. Her presence pulsed in his mind like sunlight through water.

Brandyn frowned. "What's wrong with you?"

"Just Milady showering me with her excitement," Balgair explained, smiling faintly. "If you really want to do this, you should know a few things first."

When Brandyn gestured for him to continue, the tavern's chatter dimmed, and even the fire seemed to quiet. "First, this is for life, no taksies-backsies.

What Ananke joins together, none other than death can undo."

Brandyn looked down at Lucy. "Are you worth all this trouble?"

"Yes, Maighstir, I am," Lucy whispered, eyes bright. "I will be yours forever."

Brandyn nodded, turning back to Balgair. "And the second?"

"MiLady takes a very dim view on how bonds treat each other," Balgair said, his voice deepening as the goddess's presence stirred within him. "If you use your bond to hurt your mate, Ananke will do everything in her power to make your life miserable." The tavern air grew still, warm, humming faintly like a plucked string.

"If you want to do this, and mean it, you'll have to offer your bonds to each other and accept them in return."

Lucy turned to Brandyn, crossing her wrists and lifting them. The faint shimmer of Ananke's touch illuminated the gesture, not visible light, but a subtle feeling, like awe or the edge of tears. When Brandyn took her wrists and mirrored her motion, their breath mingled.

"There before their witnesses and the gods," Balgair said softly, his voice a conduit, not his own, "they offered their bonds to one another."

The goddess's joy filled the room, a weightless warmth, a sigh of contentment that fluttered through every candle flame.

"Before these witnesses and our Lady of Chains," Balgair finished, "you are now bonded together."

The fire popped softly. Somewhere beyond the tavern walls, the wind quieted. For the first time that day, peace settled, fragile, but real, in the wake of blood and chaos.

Chapter Four

The Shadow under the Stairs

The assassin crept down the stairwell that coiled like the spine of a dead serpent. Lanternlight did not reach this deep; only the faint shimmer of glyphs carved into the stone walls, wards against lesser spirits, pulsed a sullen red as he passed. Each step was a vow to silence: heel, toe, breath held until his lungs burned.

He wasn't afraid of her, per se, but he hadn't survived for thirty-three years by being stupid.In the dim, the scent of *fuil na talmhainn,* old blood and burnt rosemary, hung in the air, the unmistakable perfume of draoidheachd worked too often in one place.

As befitting his experience, each step was carefully placed so as to raise no noise. Still, sound had a way of betraying even the careful in such a place. The stair groaned once, softly, as if sighing to the weight of his sins.

Even though he moved silently as a ghost, the witch called out to him before he reached the final step. "Oh, Indigo, where is my sacrifice?"

Her voice carried like smoke, languid, invasive, curling into his ears before the words reached meaning. When he stepped into the dim light, the witch took one look at his face. "What has Brutus done this time?"

The assassin shook his head in disgust. "The fool has gotten himself killed."

He had no particular liking for the ruffian and was secretly glad to have him dead. The gods of Saorsa, he mused, had a cruel sense of balance, fools often fed the wiser.

"How did it happen?" the witch inquired as she placed her hands on the crystal ball before her. To call her a witch wasn't entirely accurate, she would have corrected him, proudly reciting her mastery of four of the seven spheres of *draoidheachd.* But to him, a witch was a witch, no matter the breadth of her arrogance.

The orb thrummed faintly beneath her touch. Silvery mist coiled upward, alive with whispering shapes. Faces flickered within it, witnesses, victims, memory itself, replaying death in miniature.

"Apparently he tracked the woman down and confronted her in the common room of the Black Swan," Indigo said. To him, the act had been folly. She should have sent him to secure the prize himself. "According to witnesses, she has a defender, and he took Brutus apart without trying."

The witch muttered a few words, and the scrying haze convulsed with color. In the orb's depths, Indigo glimpsed the brief shimmer of the inn, people falling like marionettes cut loose from their strings.

"I see," she grumbled. "He also got Darfyn killed."

Lifting her hand from the orb, she stared at the assassin, eyes lit from within by that baleful draoidheachd glow, green shot with gold, the hue of dying stars. "Come, Indigo, let's go take our sacrifice."

She stood, sweeping her cloak about her shoulders in a motion that stirred the air like wings. "We can't fail now. The great one awaits."

The assassin inclined his head, the faintest curl of a smirk ghosting his lips. "As you wish, Brigid."

Behind them, the orb flickered once more, and for the briefest instant, the reflection of a spider's web rippled across its surface, strung with dew that glowed like tiny eyes. Then it went dark, swallowing the light whole.

Balgair had excused himself from the celebration sometime past midnight, his laughter softening to a tired hum as he slipped away from the candlelight and song.

The hall behind him still rang with joy, but joy always came with exhaustion; even the gods slept after creation. Heather followed quietly, her steps light as breath, and when he closed the door, she curled herself upon the couch and drifted into slumber.

Morning came softly through the shuttered window. Dust-motes turned in the gold light, each one catching the faint shimmer of draoidhean still resting in the air. Heather stirred first. Her eyes found him in repose, the mercenary, the servant of chains, his face unguarded in sleep. A tenderness welled up in her chest, aching and pure. She rose and knelt beside him, fingers trembling as she brushed a lock of hair from his brow.

"Good morning, *mo te alanine*," Balgair murmured, waking as if from a dream. His eyes, still half-lidded, shone with a lazy affection. "Would you like me to bond with you?"

He said it gently, almost teasingly, his hand finding hers with the ease of long habit.

Heather blinked, the words striking something deep and fragile inside her. She brushed a strand of hair behind her ear, trying to steady her voice. "You're mean," she said, half smiling through her blush, echoing Lucy's jest from the night before. "Springing that on a woman before she's properly awake."

She tried to meet his gaze but faltered, retreating into a nervous laugh. "Why would you want a woman like me?"

Tears gathered but she refused to let them fall. She pulled her hand free, the tremor in her breath betraying her heart. "I'm going to get us some breakfast," she said, forcing brightness into her voice. "I'll be back."

Her smile, brave, thin, lingered in the doorway before she turned and fled.

When the latch clicked shut, silence claimed the room. Beyond it came the faint sound of a sob, muffled by the wood. Balgair exhaled slowly. "Might as well get cleaned up," he murmured, though his chest felt heavier than it had the night before.

He crossed to the basin and splashed his face with cold water drawn from the river that wound through Eola's heart. For a moment, the chill revived him, the shock of the living world.

But as he lifted his head, something unseen brushed across his skin.

It was not air. It was not light. It was the trembling edge of a *dweomer,* a ripple in the fabric of the world, like fingers plucking the strands of Ananke's web.

"What the..." he whispered, the hair on his arms rising. The sensation slid over him again, subtle as a breath and sharp as a knife. Instinct moved him. He dressed in haste, strapping on his boots and cloak before heading for the stairs.

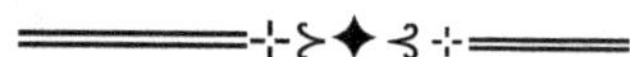

"Ready yourself, my Indigo," said the witch. Her voice was the sigh of silk over stone.

Brigid pushed open the inn's door and stepped into the pale morning. Her silver flute gleamed faintly in the half-light. When she lifted it to her lips, the sound that followed was haunting, not quite music, not quite birdsong.

It wove through the common room like mist, lilting and soft, each note a thread tugging gently on mortal minds. One by one, the early risers stilled. Heads drooped. Cups slipped from slackened fingers. The laughter of dawn gave way to silence as sleep swallowed them whole.

Indigo watched with cold admiration. Before she finished the melody, he had already slipped into the common room, his steps ghosting over the wooden floor. His eyes found the pale-haired woman at the bar, her body crumpled as if her strings had been cut.

"There you are," he muttered, a dark grin tugging at his lips. "You cost us two men. I hope you are worth it."

He slung her effortlessly over his shoulder, the way a man might heft a sack of grain. As he turned toward the door, the witch's final note lingered, high and piercing, a song of sleep and sorrow.

They had nearly reached the foyer when he heard it, the heavy rhythm of boots descending the stair, two at a time.

The spell faltered. The air itself seemed to hold its breath.

Balgair was awake.

Balgair took the stairs two at a time, his heartbeat hammering in time with the wooden rhythm. The air itself was wrong, thick, still, the silence between notes lingering like an aftertaste of enchantment. He hopped off the bottom step and ran into the common room just as the trilling notes faded into nothing.

He had expected some sort of *draoidheachd,* the residue of magic clinging to walls or light, but what he saw brought him up short. The inn looked as if a puppeteer had vanished mid-performance: every person within lay strewn across the floor, limbs slack, heads bowed. The fire still glowed, plates still steamed, but the living were as marionettes with their strings cut.

Balgair's breath hissed through his teeth. "By the Diathan—" Cursing himself for leaving his shield in the room, he drew his sword, the blackened edge whispering softly as it left the scabbard, and padded among the fallen. He moved with soldier's caution, testing for breath, for pulse, for the whisper of life.

Each body he touched was warm, each chest still rose and fell, but none stirred. They were not dead, merely stolen from waking. *Dream-theft*, he thought grimly. Old witchcraft. Old and cruel.

He counted as he went, murmuring the numbers under his breath like a ward. "Six, eight, twelve—" When he reached twenty, his search brought him to Brandyn and Lucy, collapsed behind the bar, their hands still touching as though they had fallen mid-gesture.

He frowned, scanning the room again. *No Heather.* The realization cut through him sharper than steel. He slid the sword back into its sheath and leaned over the barkeep.

"By the Diathan," Brandyn groaned, cracking open one eye and swinging at the shadow above him.

"Whoa, hold on, it's Balgair," the soldier said quickly, leaning back from the wild fist.

"Sorry," Brandyn muttered, his voice thick and weary as he tried to sit up. "All I could see was a big shadow." He half-turned and leaned back against the bar, clutching his head. "Ohh, my head—

He gathered Lucy in his arms, her fair hair spilling across his chest like spilled moonlight. "What happened in here?"

"I dunno," came the mumbled reply. "The last thing I remember was birds singing , and then you were standing over me."

Balgair's jaw tightened. "Is she—

The Tavern Master checked her pulse, nodded. Balgair sighed in relief, the tension easing only slightly. "Thank the gods. Have you seen Heather?"

"She was standing at the end of the bar, ordering breakfast." Brandyn wanted to stretch but refused to disturb Lucy. His gaze darted uneasily to the door.

Balgair snorted. "Well, she's not here now." His tone was clipped, but the look in his eyes betrayed it, fear, raw and personal.

A low moan of pain drew both men's attention downward. Lucy stirred, shaking her head. "She's gone," she whispered. "The last thing I saw before blacking out was a cloaked man carrying her out the front door."

She coughed weakly, one hand reaching up to caress Brandyn's cheek. "I'm sorry."

For the first time he could remember, Balgair felt lost. Not the battlefield kind of lost, no, this was worse. He had promised to protect Heather, and now she was gone. The oath weighed on him like cold iron. If he had just bonded her, he'd be able to find her. He knew that truth too well.

He closed his eyes. When reason failed, when fear clawed at the edges of his resolve, he did what he had always done, he reached for *Her*.

[Can you help me find Heather?]

The thought left him like a prayer cast into water.

[If you had bonded with her, you'd be able to do it yourself,] came the wry, lilting reply, the voice of Ananke, curling through his mind like warm smoke. [I understand why you didn't.]

Her tone softened the words, no scolding, just quiet understanding. Love tempered with truth.

Balgair inwardly groaned.

[You're right. I was an idiot.]

That earned him a flash of anger across his thoughts. not cruel, but bright.

[You are not an idiot, my Balgair. You're careful, and you care too much.]

Her voice folded around him like a cloak, and he could *feel* her smile in the dark of his mind.

[Give me a moment, and I'll see if I can find her.]

He waited, still as prayer. The faint hum of divine thought thrummed behind his eyes. Then, warmth. Presence. *Her touch.* It was like standing beneath sunlight after days of rain.

But with it came something else: fear. The kind he hadn't felt since his youth. The knowing that time was slipping through his fingers like spilled sand.

[If you don't relax, you're going to hurt yourself,] the Lady of Chains teased him, amused. [I've found her, and I can guide you there.]

Her next words came with gentle mischief, a goddess's mercy wrapped in humor.

[Would you like to talk to her?]

[Of course I would!]

He nearly shouted it aloud, earning a startled glance from Brandyn.

Ananke's laughter was a chime in his soul.

[You can talk to her now, and she can answer you.]

[I could hug you,] he thought fiercely, every word charged with gratitude.

He could almost see her roll her eyes, could almost *feel* her wave him off.

Then came the stillness again, deep and resonant. He closed his eyes and reached into that bond that was not yet a bond, the half-thread between their souls, alive and trembling.

[Heather?]

The assassin burst through the inn's front door, the hinges shrieking as he crossed the threshold into the cold dawn. His breath came sharp, ghosting through the chill, and the woman slung over his shoulder hung limp as if the soul had already been drawn from her. "Heather," he muttered under his breath, not her name as a person, but as a thing of value now taken. "Get a move on, Brigid. Someone is still awake in there."

The witch blinked, startled from her calm, and cursed beneath her breath. "That's not possible. The flute is an artifact." Her eyes flicked back toward the doorway, where faint light spilled like accusation.

Indigo shifted Heather's weight, the unconscious woman's hair trailing like golden silk down his back. "I heard someone running down the stairs. Maybe whoever it is, has an artifact of his own."

Brigid's lip curled, though her face remained pale beneath the hood. "It's always possible." Her voice trembled just once, the smallest crack in her certainty. She stepped into the hastily scrawled circle that marred the frost-dark earth, kneeling at its heart.

With an almost reverent motion, she pricked her right finger, letting blood drip onto the runes etched into the dirt.

"Mar a thuiteas m' fhuil,

Chun an taobh eile tha mi a' gairm,

Fosgail an t-slighe,Gu mo dhachaigh,

tha mi ag ràdh."

As my blood falls,

To the other side I call,

Open the path,To my home

I speak.

The words thrummed like harpstrings pulled too tight. The air warped, folding in upon itself; the runes began to smolder with a hungry light, leeching life from the ground and frost alike.

The smell of iron and ozone filled the space, and shadows lengthened toward her like supplicants.

A ring of darkness formed beneath them, not a hole, but a reflection too deep to be seen through. For a heartbeat, Indigo thought he saw eyes staring back from within, the suggestion of a great spider's shape, ancient and patient. Then the world gave way.

The circle collapsed. The three fell through the shadow like stones through water and landed hard upon the smooth stone of another place, another circle, drawn in the mirror image below.

Brigid rose first, brushing her fingers across the runes that still glowed faintly beneath her boots. "We're here, my Indigo," she whispered, her voice echoing through the gloom.

She lifted her left hand, and her fingers caught the last breath of magic still clinging to the air. "Ignis."

At the word, every candle on the candelabra sprang to life in a silent burst. The flames burned blue at their roots and gold at their tips, casting long, swaying shadows that made the chamber seem alive. Their light fell upon a table in the center of the lair, a crystal ball resting atop it like a heart that refused to die.

"Feel free to drop her anywhere."

Indigo obeyed without hesitation, lowering Heather onto the cold flagstones. The moment her body touched the floor, the runes around the circle pulsed once more, faintly, greedily, as if the lair itself had tasted something it liked.

The witch turned, satisfied. The portal's light flickered once, then went out, leaving only the candlefire and the echo of her god's unseen laughter.

[Heather!]

The voice echoed through the long corridors of her unmade mind, distant and trembling like the sound of a prayer lost to the wind. The unconscious woman stirred, her spirit adrift in the dim threshold between waking and dying. The air around her was heavy, thick as water, and each breath felt as though it filled her mouth with wet sand.

[Can you hear me?]

The call came again, faint and urgent, a thread cast across the void. She tried to grasp it, to shape words, but her thoughts moved sluggishly, sinking beneath the surface of sleep.

Far away, Balgair gasped. The tether between them had tightened, then gone slack. He felt the slip, the weight of her soul sinking deeper into shadow.

[I can't hear her, Milady.]

The scent of rosemary filled the air, sweet and heavy, a reminder of sacred binding and oaths fulfilled. Warm hands came to rest upon his shoulders, and the world softened at their touch. The mercenary bowed his head as if in temple, for the goddess had come.

[I can still see her,] Ananke murmured, her voice like silk drawn across iron. [But she is being shielded from you.]

He felt her lean close, breath warm upon the back of his neck, a whisper made of eternity.

[Would you like me to guide you?]

[If it pleases, Milady,] he whispered, his voice barely more than the echo of a vow.

[Then awaken and follow my lead.]

The scent of rosemary shifted, sliding from spirit to world, from prayer to place, settling like smoke upon the inn's foyer.

Balgair opened his eyes. The light of the waking world returned, duller, colder, but real. His heart still thrummed with divine rhythm. He rose slowly, feeling the chains of devotion tighten around his chest. Whoever, whatever, had shielded Heather had power enough to rival a goddess.

He would need steel.

He turned toward his room. "Where are you going?" Brandyn's voice broke the stillness.

"To get my things," Balgair said, steady and resolved. "I'm going after Heather."

"Oh?" The barkeep lifted Lucy gently, helping her sit. "Do you know where she's at?"

"No, but Ananke does." His eyes gleamed with that faint, impossible certainty only the blessed carried. "She's going to guide me."

Brandyn nodded, though unease shadowed his expression. "Here's hoping Huitzilopochtli watches over him," he muttered.

Five minutes later, the mercenary returned. The scent of iron and old blood hung about him, the relics of battle not yet washed away. The dried stains across his chainmail caught the firelight, dark as memory.

"If I were your commanding officer," Brandyn grumbled, eyeing him, "I'd yell at you for wearing bloody armor. It's borderline disgraceful."

Balgair's mouth twitched with faint shame. "I know. Believe me, I know. But I can't spare the time to clean it. I've got to save Heather."

Lucy looked up, her voice trembling. "Be careful, Maighstir. I'm not sure, but I think the spellcaster was Brigid."

Brandyn blinked. "Are you sure?"

"There are rumors," Lucy murmured, "that she can use music to cast spells."

"I'll keep that in mind," Balgair said, grasping Brandyn's forearm, a warrior's promise. "Take care of her, brother. Women like her are a gift from the gods."

Lucy smiled, radiant as dawn, curling into Brandyn's chest. The barkeep returned the clasp, mortal strength meeting divine purpose.

"Good luck on finding your girl."

Balgair inclined his head once, the faintest shimmer of rosemary trailing after him as he stepped toward the door. Somewhere, far beyond mortal sight, the Lady of Chains smiled, and the air trembled with the promise of pursuit.

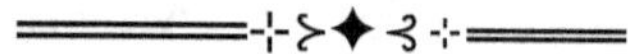

"We'll have none of that," a feminine voice said, the sound curling through the dark like smoke through incense. The syllables carried power, honeyed and cruel, as a sigil of ash and light bloomed across Heather's brow. The mark burned cold , the kind of chill that whispers to the soul instead of the skin.

Heather's body remained still, but her spirit strained. Locked within her own mind, she could hear the soft rustle of cloth, the measured movement of feet across ritual lines. Somewhere beyond the veil of her half-consciousness, someone was carving intent into the bones of the earth.

But she had heard him, *Balgair.* Hadn't she? That voice, reaching for her through the dark, it had been real. She clung to it like a drowning woman to a thread of light. Tears slipped free, shining trails that caught what little glow lingered in the circle.

"What's wrong, little one?" The voice crooned again, motherly in sound but empty of love. "You'd like to see what's going on, wouldn't you?"

Of course she would. And when the woman's steps ceased, when the sigil on her forehead shifted and the binding reformed, her eyes fluttered open. The world bled into view.

What she saw did not inspire hope. The chamber was swathed in shadows that writhed like living things, pulling away only from the circle that held her. In the weak, circling light, the runes glowed faintly, veins of a world gone wrong. She managed to roll to one side, her breath coming shallow, the symbols of the circle pulsing around her like a heartbeat not her own.

"Why," she croaked. A cough wracked her chest. "Why?"

"Why what?" the woman replied.

Heather turned her gaze upward, and met eyes of a green so deep it might have been the ocean before the first dawn. The woman standing above her was young, her crimson hair cascading like a wound come to life.

"Why are you here? Why have we kidnapped you? Why are you tied up in a magic circle?" Brigid's smile glinted sharp as a blade. It might have been lovely if not for the frost behind it, a beauty carved from cruelty.

Heather coughed again, her throat raw. "Yes, to all of those."

The smile grew feral, almost delighted. "You are here because I need a sacrifice to power the spell that will release my god from his prison."

"Why me?" Heather asked, though her heart already knew. The answer came, as prophecy always does, from the mouth of the damned.

"Because nobody will miss you."

The witch crouched low, her hand cold and deft as it drew a rune across Heather's stomach. "You have no family, no friends, and no lovers." Each word was a hammerblow, each line of ink a nail sealing her fate.

"Aww, see now, you're all frightened," Brigid cooed. "That will make it all the sweeter when my master yanks your soul from the wheel and uses your rebirth to escape the prison He Who Watches put him in."

She traced a spiral between Heather's breasts,, the mark of the devourer. "It's a shame that Brutus took your innocence. The sacrifice would have been sweeter for it, but no matter. The Creeping Chaos will be hungry."

Her robe, black as the void before creation, seemed to drink the light from the candles. The room grew darker still.

Heather drew a breath, faint and trembling. "Only Mathair Astinmah can remove a person from the great wheel," she gasped. "Any other may only kill me."

Brigid's laughter rang out like glass breaking in a crypt. "Oh, so you believe that, do you? You are in for a surprise."

The witch let silence fall, heavy, suffocating, as if giving the doomed girl time to grasp the enormity of her insignificance. Then, softly, "The Creeping Chaos devours all, and none escapes his ravenous hunger. Not even Mathair Astinmah can save this world."

Heather closed her eyes. Her pulse fluttered weakly, like a bird's wings against the bars of a cage. She saw Balgair's face in her mind, rough, kind, worn by duty, and clung to it with everything she had left.

Please, she thought. *Let me see him again. Just once more.*

She made her vow in silence: *Anything. Anything, if only I can see another dawn.*

[Anything?]

The voice was not Brigid's. It came like a ripple across still water, patient, measured, impossible to mistake.

Heather's heart stumbled. She tried to place it, to remember whose tone held both comfort and command.

[Would you give your life to me if I save you?]

The frightened girl squeezed her eyes shut. For a heartbeat, she thought herself mad. But the voice smiled.

[No, I'm not your imagination.]

The warmth in it was real. [My Balgair calls me Milady, or Our Lady of Chains.]

Hope, fragile, luminous, flared in her chest at the sound of *his* name. She remembered his quiet faith, his prayers whispered in the dark.

The goddess who had guided him, the one he had spoken of with awe and affection, was here.

Heather opened her soul like a door and offered everything she was.

[Welcome, mo te àlainn,] came the answer, rich and tender as sunlight through stained glass. [I knew I was right about you.]

The weight of divinity settled around her, not crushing but enveloping. The cold of the circle receded as warmth spread through her veins, golden, steady, alive.

For a moment, she was not in that lair but within something vast, something eternal. The goddess's arms wrapped her in invisible chains made not of iron, but of promise.

She wanted to stay there, to drown in that gentleness, but the sensation began to fade.

[Don't worry,] Ananke murmured as her presence dimmed like twilight receding from dawn. [Balgair is on his way.]

Balgair followed the scent of rosemary into the waking dark. It threaded through the night like a memory, thin and deliberate, drawing him out through the inn's door and onto the cobbled street beyond.

The wind shifted, and the fragrance moved with it , left, then further still, as though the goddess herself were walking just ahead, unseen.

At the corner, the trail faltered. The night deepened, the lamps hissed. He closed his eyes and listened, not with his ears but with the place inside where prayer takes root.The scent resumed, faint but stubborn, leading him to a narrow alley where waste and shadow slept together.

"Now what?" he muttered, his breath forming ghosts that hovered before his lips. He could taste the damp on the air, the rot beneath the stones. "You've got to be kidding me."

Still, he went on. That is what faith does, it demands movement even when the road stinks of the grave.

He walked softly, the soles of his boots whispering across filth. Each step drew him deeper, each heartbeat a wordless supplication to the Lady of Chains.

The rosemary veered right. Balgair turned, and there it was: a door, half-sunken into the wall of a forgotten building. Its wood was swollen with years and lies.

He paused, studying the structure, the slanted brickwork, the windows bricked over from within, the silence too complete to be natural. He could almost hear the pulse of the place, a rhythm that did not belong to the living.

At last he muttered, "To ifrinn with it."

He set his shield before him, the sigil of Ananke faintly glowing beneath the grime, and stepped toward the door. Raising his left hand, he knocked.

"Who be it?" came a muffled voice, hoarse and suspicious. "What business have ye?"

For a moment, Balgair considered truth. He imagined saying, *I am a soldier of the Lady of Chains, and I come for the captive you stole.*

But truth has its own weight, and not every ear can bear it. So he said nothing.

He knocked again.

"Look here ya git, if you don't answer, you don't get in."

Balgair listened, the scrape of feet, the shift of shadow behind the wood. He measured the distance, the rhythm of the man's breath. When the time was right, he drew his sword and buried it to the hilt through the door.

There was a wet gasp, the universal sound of mortality remembering itself, then silence.

"All you had to do was open the door," Balgair muttered. His tone carried no anger, only weary ritual. He lifted his leg and kicked, hard. The door splintered inward, the dying guard collapsing in a heap of cloth and blood.

"So much for a quiet entry," he said, stepping over the body.

Inside, the air reeked of dust, incense, and stale magic. The shadows felt heavier than they should. Balgair knelt briefly beside the corpse, not to mourn, but to honor the moment. Death deserved acknowledgment, even when deserved. He wiped his blade on the man's shirt and rolled the body in the moldy carpet.

Faith is not clean work.

He carried the dead man outside and laid him in the refuse, whispering, "Go find your peace, if the gods still hear you." When he returned, the scent of rosemary brushed past him again, lighter now, as though approving his grim resolve.

Pulling his cloak close, he moved down the corridor. Each door he passed held its own secrets , some whispered, some groaned. The walls sweated moisture, and the candlelight dripped in uneven pools.

He kept his steps steady, sword at ease, heart alert. Those few who passed gave him no trouble, perhaps sensing something coiled in him that was not to be tested.

He asked questions where he could, quiet, deliberate. *A witch. A blond woman. Short blue dress.* Faces turned pale. Heads shook. Silence spread like contagion.

Doubt crept in, *Was this even the right place?* When one door opened ahead. A woman emerged, bare-skinned and trembling in the half-light. Her eyes widened at the sight of him.

"Shhh," he said softly, shaking his head. "I'm looking for a blonde-haired woman wearing a short blue dress, a witch, or both."

She hesitated. Fear flickered in her gaze, but so did something else, pity, perhaps.

"If you can help me, I'll let you go," Balgair continued. "You can either get back inside that room or run out the front door. Do you know where she is?"

He didn't expect an answer. But the woman pointed, hand trembling, toward the far end of the hall.

"She's down there. She lives in the basement," she whispered, before retreating into her room, the door closing like the last note of a prayer.

"Goddess bless you," Balgair murmured, pressing forward.

His eyes traced every door he passed, ready for violence. But the corridor remained still, save for the throb of old pipes and unseen lives. Each closed door felt like a reprieve.

Then , movement.

The door creaked open. A figure cloaked in gray stepped out, blocking his path.

"You don't belong here." The stranger's tone was low, assessing. "Earl would have never let you in."

Balgair's face betrayed nothing. "I don't know what you're talking about. When I got here, the door was standing wide open."

"Unlikely," the man said, his hand slipping into his cloak. Two daggers gleamed in the half-light like hungry eyes. "Earl would never abandon his post. He gets paid a lot to stop trouble."

"Guess he took the money and split," Balgair replied, his grip tightening around his sword.

"Again, unlikely," the man said flatly. "I don't know who you are, but you aren't going any further."

Balgair sighed softly, drawing his sword. The steel sang, low, cold, almost reverent. "What's more important, your life, or hers?"

The man's brow lifted. "Mine, of course. Which is why I must stop you. If I don't try, my soul will be devoured."

He stepped into a guarded stance, one dagger raised, one poised low, the stance of a desperate man serving a merciless god.

And there, in the stale air of that forsaken hall, the light of Ananke's follower met the shadow of another faith.

Two souls bound by chains, two creeds of fear, two hearts that had long forgotten mercy.

The goddess watched in silence, somewhere just beyond the veil, as her chosen lifted his blade.

The air before the duel held a pulse, faint, metallic, and alive. Rosemary hung like incense, ghosting through the corridor as though the Lady herself watched unseen from the shadowed rafters.

Balgair's breath was slow, measured, the rhythm of a prayer turned inward. His shield settled on his arm with a whisper of chain against leather. "I don't want to kill you," he said, his voice a vow rather than warning. "All I want is the girl back."

The cloaked man's silence answered him. The stillness had the density of choice, a soul balancing on the edge of damnation. Then that sharp smile, the look that promised death. "Very well," Balgair murmured, lowering his stance. "Let's have at it."

The first clash was thunder in a narrow hall. The Black Swan surged forward, shield striking like a sermon, the word of faith made flesh. The man reeled, recovered, and came again, twin daggers gleaming like black stars. They met in a flurry of movement too fast for thought, steel striking steel, sparks glancing off the walls like scattered prayers.

The air shuddered around them. Each step, each pivot, was liturgy:

The assassin rolled past him, the daggers flashing. Balgair turned, pivot smooth as breath, shield up just as the next strike came for his back.

The clang filled the hall; the Lady's sigil flared faintly where the dagger met the iron boss, the scent of rosemary deepening as if she approved.

"Not bad," the other said, and his tone held almost admiration. "You aren't a common crook," Balgair replied, steady, sword low but alive in his hand.

The duel became language. Words were blades, and blades were words. Each thrust answered, each blow countered, until motion itself blurred into chant. The stranger's movements were honed desperation; Balgair's, tempered mercy.

When the mercenary drove his shield forward again, the air rippled like a heartbeat. The man stumbled, laughing under his breath, laughter that carried the exhaustion of too many deaths. "You might be right," he said, and shed his cloak like a serpent sloughing off old skin.

The black leather beneath devoured the light. It was not forged; it was grown, living armor, whispering with the pulse of a darker god. The air dimmed around it.

"Is that Iron-Leaf leather?" Balgair asked, though his voice came from somewhere deeper, half wonder, half mourning.

The man smiled. "I am Indigo Yarsmith, and you killed my father." A pause, then a cruel chuckle. "No, not really , but it sounded good."

The levity rang hollow, a jest to hide the gnawing in his soul. Then he moved.

The sword in one hand, the sheath in the other, his dance changed rhythm. He struck low and fast, the sheath hooking beneath Balgair's shield, the sword arcing down like judgment. The Black Swan twisted his wrist, caught the steel, and locked it there, a cruciform struggle, the symbols of two gods grinding against one another.

"I wasn't recruited yesterday," Balgair growled, and shoved him back.

"You're becoming quite the challenge," Indigo grunted, sweat and shadow streaking his jaw. Then he whistled , three short notes, sharp as cuts.

From the hall's darkness came footsteps, the ring of steel, the whisper of loaded crossbows. Three figures joined him, one bearing the cruel gleam of a bec de' corbin, the others crouched low with their bolts trained.

The corridor tightened around them, heavy with dread. But still, the scent of rosemary lingered. The Lady watched. Her chain-bearer stood his ground.

Balgair shifted his stance. The light from a guttering lantern fell across his face, catching the reflection of Ananke's mark etched faintly in his armor's surface, a sigil half-seen, half-remembered. His voice was low, almost tender. "I gave you the chance to walk away," he said. "Now, the gods decide who leaves this place breathing."

The assassin smiled, but his eyes flickered, haunted. Somewhere in that gaze, a trapped thing clawed for mercy it no longer believed existed.

And as they closed upon him, the air thickened, the shadows swayed, and every heartbeat became a drumbeat of the divine.

Steel rang. Sparks fell like fireflies. And over it all, the faint, steady hum of the goddess's chain, unseen, unbroken, wrapped the hall in its unseen rhythm.

The corridor breathed around them, damp air, old dust, and the faint scent of rosemary, ghosting like incense from a chapel unseen. Somewhere, the Lady of Chains watched, her gaze heavy as moonlight, patient as time.

"Well, crap," the Black Swan muttered, quietly assessing the danger.

The bec de' corbin was a cruel thing. The haft shortened for hallways, the pike lean and gleaming like a serpent's tooth. The hammer head and spike opposite it were the true menace , one to break, one to pierce. A weapon forged for judgment, perverted now into execution.

He shifted his weight, lowering his center, his stance that of a man who had fought too many battles to ever trust mercy.

As long as he kept Yarsmith and the bec wielder out of reach, he might live through this. The crossbowmen were danger of another kind, patient, waiting for the smallest lapse in faith.

"No offense, stranger, but I just had to call some friends out to play," Yarsmith said as he stepped to the left, his shadow peeling away from him as if unwilling to share the space.

Balgair said nothing. He watched the four men, realizing from their silent alignment that they had fought together before, not allies by affection, but by habit and coin. The mercenary adjusted his shield, drawing it close to his chest, feeling its battered face tremble faintly with each heartbeat.

He had already chosen. The first would be the one who bore the bec de' corbin. It was always better to silence the loudest threat.

He lunged forward, quick and low, driving the tip of his sword toward the man's belly. It was a killing strike, precise, efficient, merciless. The kind of move born from too many winters and too little faith left to waste on words.

But the man twisted, narrow as a whip. The sword glanced past him. His answering growl was deep, animal, and he dropped the bec's head low, the weapon aimed like accusation at Balgair's heart. Then, with a piston's snap, he drove it forward.

The clang of steel on iron echoed like a struck bell. Balgair winced as the pike gouged a line across his shield, dissecting the painted Black Swan. For an instant, the sigil split, faith wounded but unbroken, and the scent of rosemary flared sharp, bright, burning.

He slid back two steps, shaking his numbed arm, his breath ragged.

"That won't work," he murmured, voice half-prayer, half-warning. He took a step back, eyes flicking between targets. Yarsmith lingered at the rear, calculating. The crossbowmen angled for open shots. The bec wielder, steady, silent, advanced again.

This one did not waste breath on taunts. He raised the maul-like head to his shoulder, hands gripping the haft like a smith before the forge. The motion was simple, brutal. When he swung, the air cracked, and pain bloomed across Balgair's arms as the hammer struck the shield's center. He was pushed back five steps, boots scraping against the stone, the breath ripped from his chest. His wrists screamed their protest, but he held.

Light flared, a glint of intent rather than mercy, and he almost didn't get the shield up in time. A crossbow bolt slammed against it, sparking and tumbling away. The mercenary's gaze never left the bec wielder, who wound up for another strike.

He couldn't take too many more. The arm was already trembling. The chain of his goddess, unseen but felt, hummed faintly along his spine, reminding him that faith, too, was a kind of armor.

He feigned weakness, staggering a step backward, hiding strength beneath pain. He angled himself toward the nearest corner, where he could brace against the wall and make their circle narrower. He knew his body well enough to lie with it convincingly.

But the gods test the proud. He forgot the crossbowmen. The next bolt hissed low, slicing across his knee, a white-hot line of pain that tore a grunt from his throat.

While his attention flickered, the bec wielder struck again, silent and perfect. The underhanded swing caught the shield at a crooked angle, the blow twisting him off his feet. The world tilted. He crashed to the floor, the breath knocked clean out of him.

For a heartbeat, he saw the ceiling above, dark, cracked plaster, threads of cobweb trembling in the draft. The air pulsed with dull echoes of combat, every sound distant and hollow.

Then, through that haze, came the faintest whisper, not from his enemies, but from the goddess herself. [*Still you stand.*]

He rolled to one side, dragging himself to one knee. His body hurt, but the chain in his soul thrummed steady. He hunched behind his shield, the wounded swan glaring up at the four shadows before him. Each breath was a vow, each heartbeat a prayer unspoken.

The mercenary of the Black Swan was not done yet.

The corridor had grown too still. The smell of iron and old dust hung heavy, yet beneath it lingered a softer scent, rosemary and burnt air, the perfume of his goddess. It wrapped around him like a memory of safer days.

"Of all the stupid things you've done," Balgair cursed under his breath, "this has to be in the top two." His words fell flat against the stone, small and mortal.

Rhyslin would have kicked his ass for this, Marcus too. "Dumb, dumb, dumb," he muttered, hearing in his head Rhyslin's slow, disbelieving sigh and Marcus's low growl of disapproval. He knew what they'd say: *Never go in alone. Never without your men*

But he hadn't been thinking like a soldier. He'd been thinking like a man who loved, and in Saorsa, that kind of thinking was as dangerous as any blade.

He could retreat, but that would mean leaving Heather to die. Reinforcements would take weeks to reach Eola, and the trail would be cold long before they arrived. He could ask Rhyslin or Marcus for help, and they'd come, but every favor owed chained the soul a little tighter. A man in Saorsa stood on his own, or he bartered pieces of himself to stand with others. He could talk to Brandyn, but that, too, would come at a cost.

And then there were the gods.

He thought of Ananke, his Lady, his Milady, but she was not a god of war. Her sphere was oaths, contracts, the invisible bonds that held men and gods alike to their word. Her gifts lay in threads, not blades.

Mixcoatl? No. This wasn't the hunt. Quetzalcoatl? This wasn't defense or wisdom.

That left one. Huitzilopochtli, forger of strength, bringer of courage, lord of the field and the bleeding sun. Balgair had never prayed to him before, a soldier without a war god, a mercenary who had never offered the blood that bought divine favor. If irony were a coin, he could have paid his debt tenfold.

He looked up. The four shadows before him shifted closer, weapons gleaming. The bec wielder smiled, a cruel, knowing curve of the mouth that promised more pain. The air trembled with their hunger.

There was a door behind him. Twenty feet. Too far.Another, ten feet away. Maybe luck, maybe providence.

"Are you still alive, Black Swan?" Yarsmith called. "I'd hate for you to die before we finished our fight."

Balgair did not answer. He pressed his lips together and bowed his head for the briefest heartbeat. [*Forgive me, Milady,*] he prayed in silence. [*I screwed up, and put Heather's life at risk. I need some help. Any you can give would be appreciated.*]

The air answered. It didn't roar or shine, it *shifted.* The light dimmed to twilight; the scent of rosemary deepened until it filled his lungs like prayer. Then smoke rose from the cracks between stones, slow, deliberate, curling upward in elegant spirals.

It wasn't fire-born. It was *contract-born.* Every tendril a signature of her will.

The smoke gathered between him and the enemy, thickening into a veil of gray. The crossbowmen coughed, confused, their forms lost in the haze.

The hammer wielder cursed, eyes watering. Only Yarsmith stood still, suspicion flickering behind his mask of confidence.

Balgair did not wait for their recovery. He turned and ran, each step echoing like a heartbeat against the walls. The world beyond the smoke seemed strangely clear, as though Ananke had marked a path only he could see.

He tried the first door, locked. The second gave way beneath his hand. He dove through, slamming it behind him, the latch catching like a sigh. He could jam it, but that would trap him. Better to move.

[*Thank you, Milady,*] he whispered aloud, the words trembling in his throat. The air was cooler here, untouched by smoke or blood.

He passed through another doorway and found himself in a dark vestibule. Dust motes drifted in narrow shafts of moonlight through cracked boards. He waited, one breath, two, three, listening for pursuit. None came.

His legs gave way beneath him. He sank to his knees, pressing his forehead against his shield. The gouge across the swan's body stared back at him like a wound that would not heal.

"Great Huitzilopochtli, forger of strength and bringer of courage," he whispered, each word steadying his shaking breath. "I need help. I have not called upon you, and you may reject me. However, what I seek is for someone else. One of Ananke's daughters is being held captive and will be sacrificed to the Creeping Chaos unless I can free her."

His words faded into stillness. Then the air changed again.

It began as a tremor beneath his skin, the pulse of a drum far away, echoing through the marrow.

The scent of rosemary receded, replaced by something sharper: blood, copper, sunlight on iron. A warmth spread across his shoulders, pressing down, heavy as a warrior's hand.

He knew, without seeing, that the War God had come.

Silence filled the vestibule, thick, alive. The god did not speak at first. His awareness swept outward, like fire crawling across dry grass.

Balgair felt it moving through walls, through minds, through hearts, testing the pulse of the living, tasting the fear that drifted from room to room.

And then, the words, not sound, but *knowing*.

[*Very well, you will have my help. Stand fast, chain-maker, for help will soon be there.*]

The title struck through him like thunder muffled by reverence. *Chain-maker.* Not mercenary. Not soldier. Something forged between.

Balgair exhaled, the tension spilling from his limbs. He leaned back against the wall, eyes closing. The cold stone steadied him; the divine warmth lingered, a heartbeat against his spine.

For the first time since Heather's abduction, he allowed himself to breathe without fear. Smoke still lingered in his hair, the perfume of his goddess. The air around him thrummed faintly with the war god's presence, patient and watchful.

He sighed, exhaustion and gratitude folded together. "Thank you," he whispered, though he wasn't sure which god he meant.

And for a long while, there was peace in the dark,the silence before the next storm.

Chapter Five

The Clarion Call

The morning light seeped through the warped glass of *The Black Swan's* windows, silvering the dust motes that hung motionless in the air. The tavern was still, too still, as if time itself had been lulled by the witch's song. Somewhere, beneath the silence, a faint breath of rosemary lingered, the echo of a goddess who had watched her children fall into enchanted sleep.

Brandyn stood at the center of the common room, eyes roaming across the sprawled shapes of his patrons. His count faltered at a dozen. *So many,* he thought, his heart tightening. "Come on, Lucy." His voice broke the stillness. "We have to see who's dead and who's alive."

Lucy disentangled herself from his arms, shivering. The air still carried a chill that wasn't natural. "How many do you suppose are dead?" she asked, brushing her arms as though to shake off unseen eyes.

"Hopefully none," the barkeep muttered, stepping away from the safety of the bar. His boots creaked on the floorboards that had seen laughter, song, and spilled ale the night before. Now they only whispered. He knelt beside the nearest man, placed two fingers against his throat , and sighed as warmth still pulsed beneath his skin. "This one's alive." He adjusted the body reverently, folding the man's arms as one might a fallen comrade.

Lucy mirrored him at the next table. "So is she." Her voice was steadier now, anchored by hope.

It took them twenty long minutes to move among the bodies, twenty minutes of breath and silence of heartbeats slowly returning to rhythm. When they met again by the bar, Brandyn leaned against the counter, shoulders heavy. "Ten men, eight women. All alive , just asleep." He frowned, rubbing the back of his neck. "Do you remember how many guests we had?"

Lucy shook her head. "No, Maighstir. Should we check upstairs?" She didn't want to, not with that strange quiet pressing down like snowfall, but she already knew the answer.

"It couldn't hurt," he said, and started for the stairs. "Better to check and find them all alive, than find a dead body later."

His mouth twitched into a weary smile. "If you don't want to search upstairs, you can stay down here."

Lucy's eyes widened. "Stay here, with all them looking like that? Nope." She shook her head frantically. "I'm going with you."

They climbed together. The floorboards creaked beneath their steps, the only sound besides their breathing.

Upstairs, the rooms smelled faintly of lavender soap and spilled cider, and every door they opened revealed only stillness and the soft, steady rise and fall of sleeping chests. When they came back down, relief sat heavy in their limbs, a kind of exhausted grace.

At the bar again, Brandyn poured them both a drink. "All alive," he murmured. The words should have comforted him. Instead, they hung hollow. He raised his cup halfway to his lips , and froze. "Did you hear that?"

Lucy blinked. "Hear what?" She looked at him, concern softening her face. "The only thing I hear is their breathing." She gestured to the sleepers along the wall, half joking.

Brandyn frowned. "I thought I heard a war horn."

"Are you sure you aren't hearing the flute from earlier?" Lucy teased gently, pressing her palm to his forehead as though checking for fever.

He brushed her hand away, growling low. "No, what I heard wasn't a flute. It sounded like a war horn."

Something in his tone silenced her. The air shifted again, the faintest hum in the rafters, like the after-ring of metal struck upon metal. Then Lucy, hesitant, changed the subject with a question that had lingered since their bonding. "Maighstir," she said softly, "now that you've bonded me, what are you going to expect from me?"

Her earnestness startled him. He took a slow breath, searching for words. "I expect you to continue to do your job. Serve our patrons as if you are serving me, and always be on your best behavior." He caught her hands and placed them against his heart, a gesture both simple and binding.

The barmaid blushed. "What if I misbehave?" she asked, eyes bright with a teasing hope.

Brandyn lifted a brow. "If you misbehave, I will have to punish you."

She smiled at that, a woman finally at peace with the strength of the man she'd chosen. "Will you ever expect me to dance for our patrons?"

He blinked, taken off guard. Scratching his chin, he frowned. "Maybe."

The sound came again, faint, distant, unmistakable. *A war horn.* This time, Lucy heard it too. It rolled through the inn like thunder's breath, and the glasses on the shelves trembled in their hooks. Brandyn's eyes widened. "That sounds almost like a Clarion Call."

Almost as if the horn had summoned them, the front door burst open. Two men stormed in, breathless, their boots striking the wood with purpose. One wore a cloak of restless colors, hues chasing each other like wind over water; the other, a ranger in black and tan, plucked the string of the bow slung over his shoulder.

"Brandyn, was that a Clarion Call I heard?" the first demanded.

Brandyn blinked, still leaning against the bar. "Did you hear it twice?"

"Yes," said the ranger. "And there's no mistaking that sound. Only captains get Clarion Calls."

"Then there's your answer." Brandyn straightened. "There's a Black Swan captain in town. He saved Heather from Brutus."

The two men exchanged looks. Brandyn grinned. "See what happens when you don't visit daily?"

"Go on," grunted the ranger.

"We think the witch beguiled us with her music and kidnapped Heather. The captain went after her."

The men swore under their breath. "We should've hunted down Brutus and his cronies months ago."

Brandyn gave them a flat look. "You two griped about it after Dafyd and his deputies were killed , then got drunk and forgot."

Silence hung a heartbeat, then the old soldier in him stirred again, that long-sleeping discipline thrumming awake. "If you two are hearing the war horn, then there's no choice but for us to help him."

He turned toward Lucy, his voice softening. "You know where I keep my leathers, right?"

She blinked in surprise but nodded.

"Go grab them. We have people to save."

Lucy stood frozen, her lips parted, no sound coming out. Brandyn hesitated, then invoked the one truth that would move her heart. "He was the one who assisted us with the bonding ceremony."

The words broke her hesitation like glass.

"Yes, Maighstir."

Lucy was gone in a flurry of skirts, light-footed as a promise kept. Her steps rang up the stairwell, the soft thunder of devotion.

Brandyn stood still for a breath. The silence that followed was not silence at all—it was charged, humming faintly, as though the gods themselves inhaled with him. Behind him, the two men who had answered the call adjusted their cloaks, faces drawn taut with recognition. For the first time in many years, *The Black Swan* was no longer just a tavern, it was a garrison waking from slumber.

Somewhere in the marrow of the world, a god's horn still echoed. The note hung over the town like a dream of war, like a warning to the righteous heart.

Brandyn turned from the sound and reached above the bar. His fingers closed around the haft of the war-axe. The iron whispered against the wood as he pulled it down, the edge catching light like dawn on old steel.

He turned next to the wall, where his shield hung—painted with three chevrons, the mark of a man who had once carried command. When he lifted it from its hooks, dust fell away like a benediction.

While he waited for the tavern maiden's return, Brandyn tested the edge of the axe with the pad of his thumb. Still sharp. Still ready. So was he.

"Here you go, Maighstir," Lucy's voice came from behind, small and breathless but steady. She held the folded leathers in both arms as though bearing a holy relic.

Brandyn nodded his thanks. The armor creaked as he pulled it over his head, the scent of oiled hide and smoke rising like incense. The tunic was a bit tight, his years at the bar had not been kind, but it would hold.

The leather pants followed, fastened over linen. He flexed his knees, testing the fit. The old gear remembered him.

Before he could turn, Lucy wrapped her arms around him, trembling. "Maighstir, please be careful. I don't want to lose you." Brandyn froze, the war-axe heavy in his hand.

She looked up at him through wet lashes, courage and fear braided together in her eyes. Then, before doubt could still her, she kissed him—fierce, clumsy, full of everything she could not say.

"If anything happens to you," she whispered, "I don't know what I'll do."

The tavern master coughed and stepped back, daring the two men to laugh. Neither did. They only bowed their heads, as if witnessing something sacred.

Brandyn ruffled her hair gently. "I'll be careful, I promise. When I return, we'll consummate this bond."

That promise hung between them like a prayer.

Then the soldier in him reawakened. He rested the axe upon his shoulder, hefted the shield, and started for the door. "Come on, guys, let's go. We have a captain to rescue."

"Right behind ya, Lieu," the two men echoed as they fell into step. Their boots struck the floorboards like the slow heartbeat of fate.

Outside, the street was washed in the faint blue of dawn, the world holding its breath between fear and hope. Brandyn glanced down the lane. "Do you remember what direction the call came from?"

The ranger pointed north. "That way."

And they went—three men walking toward war, each with the shadow of a god at his back.

Far away, in the labyrinth below the town, Balgair listened to the muffled clamor of men searching for him. His body was bruised, his breath thin, yet his heart was steady. He knelt in the darkness, speaking softly.

"Thank you, Lord Huitzilopochtli. I will try to bring you honor."

The words felt foreign in his mouth. He had never prayed to the War-God before; he was no zealot, no glory-hunter. He had joined the Black Swans out of necessity, not zeal. What began as a six-month contract had stretched into years, a lifetime of blades and sleepless roads. His two bonds still waited on the small farm he'd meant to return to.

He bowed his head, voice raw. "But why would you help me, a man who doesn't glory in war?"

The air shifted. The stone beneath him seemed to breathe. Then came a weight, not crushing, but absolute.

When he lifted his eyes, he stood atop a mountain beneath a red sky. Two armies clashed in the valley below, their banners like bleeding stars.

"What the ifrinn..." he muttered, reaching instinctively for his sword.

"Your thoughts bring you honor," said a voice behind him—deep, calm, inexorable.

Balgair turned and froze. The god before him was carved from battle itself: black and red paint across his arms, eagle-beaked helm shadowing eyes like twin suns swallowed by night. His presence hummed through the air, a note too vast for mortal breath.

"Not all conflicts are great battles, Chain-maker," Huitzilopochtli said. "Some wars are fought within the soul."

The god extended a hand toward him, the gesture neither command nor blessing, but invitation. "You honor my sister by keeping your word and seeking balance. Could I do less, when you need aid?"

Balgair lowered his head, overwhelmed. "Why does everyone think that I'm a Sagarte of Ananke?" He spread his arms helplessly. "If I look like a priest, I don't see it."

The god's laughter rolled like distant thunder. "You have a singular view of what a Sagart is. You are no temple-bound monk. But you work, you keep your oaths, you mend the broken." His eyes softened. "You are a chain-maker in truth."

The words rang through Balgair's chest, echoing against the old scars of his conscience.

"You rescued those who were bound in darkness," the god continued. "You defend those who cannot defend themselves. You are not merely a servant of Ananke, Balgair, you are her reflection in flesh. Perhaps a *ridire naomh*."

The words struck him silent. A holy knight? Him?

The god seemed to sense the doubt. "You rode alone into danger to save a woman you barely know. That is no soldier's duty—it is a calling."

Balgair's throat worked. "But I can't do this alone."

"You won't," the War-God said simply. "They are gathering—the ones who believe in law and order. They will find you."

He turned his gaze toward the valley, where the battle raged on, a vision of every conflict in every age. "This world needs guardians. Have you ever thought of being a sheriff?"

Balgair blinked, startled by the earthliness of it. "But I have a Saor-Shealbh. A small farm—"

Huitzilopochtli raised one brow, voice stern now. "You have two bonds who have not seen you in five months. It is your faith in my sister that holds them. Would it not serve them better if you had roots? A stead, a purpose beyond coin?"

The words burned with quiet truth.

"Switch contracts," the god urged. "Become the leader these people need."

The mountain wind rose, hot and scented of iron. Balgair closed his eyes, feeling the weight of his years, the ache in his shoulders, the faint warmth of hope.

"I guess you're right," he whispered.

And the god smiled—the kind of smile that precedes sunrise.

Far below that celestial mountain, Brandyn and his companions moved north, following the call only the faithful could hear. And somewhere deep beneath stone and shadow, the mercenary knelt, his heart open, a chain newly forged between man and the divine.

The war horn sounded again—low, sonorous, and sure.The gods were watching. And for the first time in an age, Saorsa was awake.

The air in the witch's lair was thick with the scent of chalk, burnt myrrh, and blood—old magic. The walls, carved from ancient stone, seemed to pulse faintly in rhythm with Brigid's incantations, as though the very bones of the earth listened. Heather watched her captor move within the dim circle of light, her robes whispering like the wings of some patient carrion bird.

"Why do you worship Chaos?"

The question was soft, almost fragile, yet it cut through the silence like a blade through silk.

Brigid didn't pause in her work. The witch's brush traced slow sigils of black ink that shimmered faintly with power stolen from the leylines buried deep below.

"Why do people follow gods?"

Heather tugged against her bonds instinctively, the iron biting into her skin. The bindings were not just physical; they thrummed with something *alive* , a net of will that hummed with the breath of another world.

"I don't know. Why do people follow gods? I've never given it much thought."

Brigid's laughter was brittle and empty. It didn't sound cruel , it sounded *tired*, as though she'd been laughing at that same truth for years.

"Most people don't. For your information, I'm a follower of the imprisoned god because he's promised me power if I can break him out."

The words hung heavy, and the shadows along the walls seemed to lean closer, listening.

"And you're going to use me to break him out."

"You'll find out."

Her brush resumed its dance, painting runes that smelled faintly of blood and lightning. Each line glowed for a heartbeat, then faded, absorbed into the circle like water into thirsty soil.

Heather's voice was almost a prayer.

"Power isn't everything."

She remembered the wreckage of her past, the way she had wielded her will like a knife and cut even those who had tried to love her. Her breath trembled.

"What good is power if you use it to take lives? Who are you?"

Brigid completed another rune, the ink now moving on its own.

"Plan on taking my name to your grave, Heather?"

The witch's voice was cool, detached. When the blonde flinched, she smiled, not kindly, but knowingly.

"We know who you are, and what Brutus did to you."

Heather folded inward, her shoulders curling like wings around her heart. Memory clawed up her throat, the smell of sweat, the sound of laughter that wasn't hers, the darkness that never quite left.

"If you must know, my name is Brigid."

"I see." Her voice was quiet, but her eyes lifted with a flicker of defiance.

"Why serve chaos and death, when there are other gods to serve?"

Brigid's silver eyes caught the candlelight , cold, liquid, and ancient.

"Because I've prayed to those other gods, and none of them will give me what I want."

"What won't they give you? If you've earned it, they have to acknowledge it, don't they?"

"You'd think so, wouldn't you?"

Her voice trembled, not with doubt, but with rage suppressed for too long.

"I have mastered four of the schools of draoideachd, plus I've mastered half of Draoideachd Biase, and the arrogant men and women who sit in the council won't acknowledge the mastery. The chaos bringer has promised to teach me what I don't know."

Heather's heart clenched at the sound of longing, twisted and furious though it was.

"If you have that much power, why do you care what they think? Isn't there anyone who would acknowledge your power that they can't ignore?"

"Of course there is. If I could get Mac Draoidheachd to acknowledge my mastery, they'd have to accept it, but I can't find him, and thus, can't get the acknowledgement."

The room's torches flickered as if the name itself had weight.

The witch's obsession burned hotter than the circle she drew, a hunger not just for power, but for recognition, for *place* in the order of creation.

"And my death will bring this god of chaos, who will do what? Give you more power and force A Mathir's son to acknowledge you?"

"Exactly, little girl. Chaos has promised me that, and much more."

The light from the runes pulsed once, as if exhaling. The air tasted of copper and thunder. Heather felt the world tilt slightly, as though something vast and ancient had turned its gaze toward her.

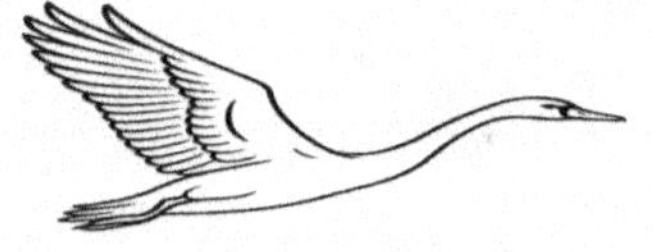

She trembled, not just from fear, but from the sudden knowing that she was standing at the hinge of something far greater than herself. She didn't want Balgair's life to be another sacrifice.

Far above, the god of war still lingered in the world of men.

The mountains were gone, but Balgair still felt their shadow, their echo pressed against his ribs. Huitzilopochtli's words burned through his mind like embers caught in wind.

"Regardless of your decision, be aware that I have found you to be a man of great character. Succeed or fail, you will make your mark."

The warmth of divine presence faded, leaving a silence so heavy it bordered on sacred.

Balgair opened his eyes. The small vestibule was still and dark, but not empty. The air shimmered faintly, like heat above a forge, and for a heartbeat he thought he could still hear the echo of wings.

"Thank you, great Huitzilopochtli, but I can't wait for your help to find me. There are some things a man must do for himself."

His voice was quiet, reverent but resolute.

He shifted from cross-legged to kneeling, the links of his mail whispering softly like prayer beads.

His fingers traced the battered face of his shield, finding each scar by touch, cataloguing every story etched into steel.

Each dent was a memory of defiance. Each scratch, a vow.

The gods might watch, he thought, *but it is mortals who bleed.*

He checked his chainmail one last time, breath steady now, spirit sharpened. Above him, faintly, he thought he heard it again, the war horn.

A divine note, carried on mortal wind.

Chapter Six

Mist and War Drums

Brandyn stepped out onto the worn flagstones and drew in a breath of the city's chill air. The wind that moved through Eola carried the tang of the river and the faint bite of coal smoke from the northern quarter.

He sighed. Once, Eola had been the pride of western Saorsa, the county seat and guardian of the hill roads, her tall limestone walls gleaming beneath banners of the old Confederacy.

Those same walls had withstood the wild years, when raiders poured out of the timberlands and war-bands stalked the trade routes.

But the Eola of today was a husk of that glory. Her walls still stood, yet within them, rot had taken root. The broad avenues, once lined with white-brick villas and shrines to the Diathan, were now pocked with burned-out taverns and shuttered shops.

When the army had built the supply depot beyond the eastern gate and raised new ramparts around it, the heart of the city had been left to fend for itself.

The thieves came first, then the assassins. They had claimed the abandoned homes and turned them into flop houses, dens, and bolt-holes. Even the shrines were desecrated, their altars cracked, their offerings stolen or replaced with mocking symbols to forgotten gods.

The Sheriff had tried, once. He'd ridden through these streets with banners flying and a prayer to Nan Diathan on his lips. But in time, even he had bent beneath the weight of compromise. The deal he struck with the guilds was an open wound: as long as blood didn't stain the streets, the law would turn its face away.

Petty crimes could be bought off with coin, and justice became just another market.

That uneasy peace had held, until Brutus.

Brutus, the knife-king of the northern tenements, had broken the old order. His gang carved out a kingdom of its own, and when the Sheriff and four deputies tried to end it, their bodies were left to hang from the western gate. The town guard, undermanned and outmatched, had been fighting a quiet, losing war ever since.

Then, just when the people had begun to whisper that even the gods had abandoned Eola, the Captain had arrived, a chain-maker of the Black Swans. He'd broken Brutus in the square before the tavern, and for a brief moment, the city had remembered what hope sounded like.

Now that memory was fading fast.

"We've got to hurry," the ranger commented as the war horn's call resounded in their minds once again. "That captain needs help, and quick."

The sound still hung in the back of Brandyn's skull like the echo of thunder in a storm valley, a clarion from the unseen realm, unmistakably divine.

"I know," Brandyn replied, setting the axe against his shoulder. "Where do you suppose Brutus had his headquarters?" He looked at the ranger. "Any ideas, Ben?"

The ranger shrugged. "I don't usually hang out in town, but I remember hearing something about a building to the north, right Methak?"

The archer nodded. "Yep, there was talk about finding the landlord hanging from one of the balconies." He glanced to the north. "If Farank was here, he'd know for sure."

A flicker of rueful amusement crossed Brandyn's face. *If Farank were here...* the man had a knack for finding trouble and walking out of it smiling.

"Hang on Captain, we're on the way," Brandyn whispered as he led the unlikely group behind him down the street.

They moved in silence through the alleyways of Eola, a ghostly procession lit by the dying sun and the pale lanterns above shuttered doorways. The war horn still echoed faintly through the ether, a call from the gods themselves. To a Saorsan, that sound was no mere rallying cry; it was an *invocation of bond*, the mark of divine sanction.

Then, from the shadowed mouth of an alley, a hiss broke the silence.

"Psst, hey, Lieu."

Brandyn turned, instinctively resting his hand on the haft of his axe. Two figures emerged from the darkness: the first a man wrapped in black leather, a brace of daggers gleaming faintly across his chest and a crossbow slung low across his back.

Behind him stood a woman of striking beauty, clothed in red silk that shimmered even in the gloom.

When her eyes met Brandyn's, she dropped to her knees and offered her wand. The gesture was not theatrical, it was ritual. A recognition of service, oath, and kinship under the Sigil of the Swans.

"Arien?" He vaguely recalled the woman as having been in his last company. She had been a minor enchantress who wanted to make a difference in the world. Then he looked at the man, and the stern expression and set jaw with a jagged scar jogged his memory. "Farank?"

Farank grinned, ignoring the kneeling woman. "Who else do ya think would answer a call?" He gestured behind him. "Ya remember Arien, don't ya?"

The former Black Swan nodded. "It's good to see you, scar-face." He took the offered hand and firmly shook it. "When did you bond the enchantress?" He glanced at the woman. "You can rise, Arien."

The enchantress rose to her feet, stepped toward her *maighstir*, and raised her hand to his shoulder.

The man grunted, "When I saved her from death about a year back. She pissed off some local yokel, and he was about to drown her." He released Brandyn's hand. "Bonded her right on the spot. So, who's the captain?"

Brandyn hesitated. He could almost feel the weight of his oath tugging at his tongue. But these were Swans, *kin by chain and by vow.* He took a breath, praying silently that Balgair would forgive the breach.

"His name is Balgair, and he's a current Black Swan chain-maker. The short story is that Brutus challenged him to duel over Heather."

The thief-taker and enchantress exchanged a knowing look, one of those wordless recognitions that passed among veterans of the same wars and whispers.

"The Captain killed Brutus and saved Heather. That was yesterday." He sighed. "And this morning, a spell caster using a flute ensorcelled my patrons and made off with Heather." After giving the two a moment, he continued, "The captain went after them."

He gestured behind him at the crowd. "They heard the call, so the Captain must be in trouble."

"I can tell," the thief-taker said as he looked over Brandyn's shoulder. "I see Ben and Methak." He pointed at the ranger and archer. "Yep, that should do it." He turned back to Brandyn. "You said it was bardic spell caster that hit your place, right?"

"Yes," Brandyn answered, "The last I remember was hearing the flute."

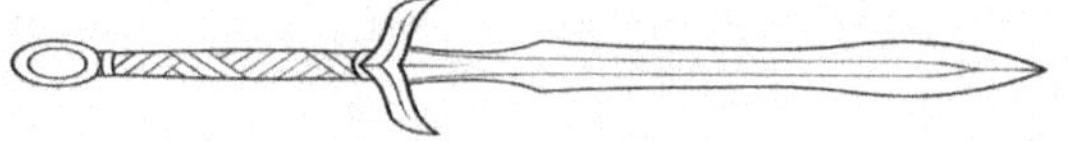

The air in the alley shifted, a low vibration, almost imperceptible, like the hum of a plucked string resonating between the worlds. Somewhere, far off yet near, a god was listening.

And Eola, tarnished and trembling, was about to remember what it meant to be free again.

The thief-taker scratched his chin and spoke to the woman behind him.

"Doesn't Brigid practice bardic magic?"

"Yes, *maighstir*, among others." The enchantress nodded as she bit her lower lip.

The thief-taker took a slow breath, eyes narrowing as memories surfaced like old scars.

"If it was Brigid, I know where she's holed up, and if your chain-maker is there, he's going to need help fer sure."

He turned and pointed to the north, where the rooftops gave way to a single crooked tower that stabbed into the smoky sky. Its silhouette seemed to drink in the dying light.

"Brigid has turned that whole building into one big house for thieves, assassins, women of ill repute, and dregs of society. They won't go easily."

The man's voice was steady, but even he hesitated a moment before adding,

"I think at last count, there were several hundred living in that building, and if they don't think they'll live, they'll go to the last man, woman, and child."

The building loomed like a black tooth above the rest of Eola, half-shrouded by smoke and prayer ash drifting from the ruined shrines nearby. Even from a distance, Brandyn could feel the place's weight , a *knot in the weave,* where dark intentions tangled and festered.

"Just great," Brandyn muttered. "Normally, that would take what, four squads of men to handle?"

The thief-taker nodded in agreement, his jaw set.

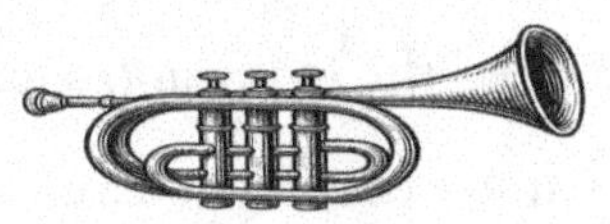

"Yep, but that was a clarion call, and Huitzilopochtli doesn't just sound that trumpet without a good reason. This captain must have friends in high places."

Brandyn met his gaze and gave a solemn nod. The sound of the horn still trembled in his chest, as though the Great War God himself stood over them, waiting to see who would rise.

"That's what I thought," the thief-taker went on, "and it won't be easy; Yarsmith lives in that building."

At the mention of the assassin's name, silence fell like a shroud. The street seemed to hold its breath. Even the stray wind quieted, as if wary of carrying that cursed name too far. Yarsmith , the shadow that stalked the living and silenced the guilty and innocent alike. Every soul present had heard the stories.

Every one of them knew the blood trail he had left through Saorsa's heart.

Brandyn turned to face the ten who stood behind him. Men and women who had seen too much, lost too much, yet still followed when the horn called. The tavern lamps flickered across their faces, carving lines of resolve and fear in equal measure.

"If you don't want to do this, you can leave," Brandyn said quietly. "The Great War God won't think badly of you."

He meant it , and in that moment, the *weight of choice* settled upon them all.

The ranger grunted, his eyes never leaving the shadowed tower.

"I owe that assassin a strike about the head. He killed a friend of mine. Isn't that right, Methak?"

The archer nodded, his voice low and tight.

"Aye, he killed Lena."

A ripple of shared pain passed through the group. The memory of old wounds has a strange way of binding souls together, and in that quiet, something unseen stirred , a current moving through them like a tide drawn by divine gravity.

Brandyn felt it too. Pride swelled in his chest, not for himself but for these broken souls who had chosen to stand. Balgair, he thought, you'd laugh to see what you've started. A band of tavern-dwellers turned heroes for a day.

The silence shattered as the war horn sounded again, closer this time, followed by the steady pulse of drums.

The sound rolled through Eola's hollow streets like thunder over stone.

The ranger looked at Brandyn, eyes wide.

"By Mixcoatl, this must be important. This isn't just about Heather. There's something greater afoot."

At the mention of the Dreaming God's name, the air itself seemed to breathe. A faint, silver mist crept from the cracks between the stones and drifted down the street, soft and luminous. It coiled around their feet, cool as river fog, yet it hummed faintly, as though alive with memory.

The archer raised a brow, awe softening his rough voice.

"If that's not Mixcoatl's blessing, then I don't know what is. You're right, Ben; I'm all in as well."

He turned to Brandyn, his face set in calm acceptance.

"Just promise me that if we fall, you'll find a way to release us to the wheel."

The Tavern Master's reply was a solemn nod.

"Good nuff for me," Methak muttered.

The mist deepened then, curling around their legs and rising to their knees. Brandyn could feel it , the pulse of the gods, the breath of Saorsa herself, stirring as her children took up arms once more.

Somewhere above the rooftops, the last light of the setting sun caught on the tower's blackened spire, and for an instant, it gleamed like tempered steel.

War had come to Eola, and the gods were watching.

Balgair spent nearly half an hour making sure his armor was sound. The dull light that filtered through the cracks in the old timbers caught on the faint scratches and dents that marked each piece , ghosts of past battles, silent witnesses to his endurance. Every buckle fastened, every strap tightened was a prayer of preparation, unspoken but felt.

He knew help was coming. He could almost *feel* them drawing nearer, like distant thunder building beneath the earth. But time in that crumbling place stretched thin, elastic with tension and silence. He didn't know how long he had, only that Heather was somewhere below, and she was waiting.

"Here goes nothing," he muttered as he rose, the quiet words almost swallowed by the walls themselves. The mercenary stepped toward the door. Beyond it, he could hear the rasping voices of Yarsmith's men prowling the corridors, their laughter cruel and hollow. Somewhere beneath their feet lay the chamber where Heather was held. He wondered how she was faring, if she still believed in him.

Heather tried to lift her hand to brush away the tears gathering in the corner of her eyes, but the weight of the chains made even that small gesture feel impossible. She didn't want the witch to see her fear. The air around her was close and heavy, thick with candle smoke and the faint scent of herbs burned to mask decay.

As her heartbeat quickened, so did the darkness within her, the old, quiet ache that whispered she was small, forgotten, unworthy. She sank back into her thoughts and reached into that hidden corner of her spirit, the place where she had last heard the goddess' voice.

[Are you still there?]

Her plea trembled through the silence. When Ananke didn't answer at once, Heather's hope faltered.

Perhaps she had imagined it all, a trick of pain and loneliness.

[I'm here, *mo neach briste.* I'll never leave you,] the goddess finally answered, her voice soft as wind through a hollow. [I will always answer when you call, but it may take a few minutes.]

Heather closed her eyes, her breath unsteady. Relief mingled with exhaustion.

[Am I going to die here?]

The question slipped from her like a confession.

[Not if we can help it,] Ananke replied, her tone both gentle and sure. [Balgair is still coming for you. He's just been delayed.]

Heather's mind reached for the image of him, the weathered face, the dark eyes that held patience even in pain.

His careworn smile. It rose clearly out of the dark like a flame that refused to die. But then fear coiled around her heart.

[He's in trouble, isn't he?]

[It's nothing, my dear,] the goddess soothed. [He's facing his equal in bladesmanship, but he'll win. He always does.]

Another face intruded, sharp eyes, a cruel grin, and her stomach turned.

[He's fighting Yarsmith, isn't he?]

The silence that followed spoke louder than denial.

[Please tell him to leave,] she begged. [Please, Mistress Ananke. I don't want him to die because of me. I'm not important enough.]

Her voice broke in the spaces between thoughts.

[He has two other women to take care of. I'm just a woman he took in out of pity.]

The words echoed hollowly in her mind. For a moment, she feared she'd driven even the goddess away, that her weakness, like a curse, might strip away even divine compassion. But then she felt warmth.

The air thickened, fragrant with rosemary and sunlight remembered. It wrapped around her shoulders like unseen arms.

[Why are you giving up?] Ananke asked softly, her tone laced with a faint, loving reproach.[Do you lack faith in my Balgair?]

Heather shook her head, trembling, ashamed.

[I have worked very hard to get the two of you together, so don't give up on him.]

The voice shimmered like laughter under moonlight, strange, maternal, and eternal. Heather didn't understand. She wasn't meant to.

[Why me? I'm nobody,] she whispered inwardly.[Not even my friends tried to help me.]

The presence drew closer, like the warmth of a fire after long cold.

[That can be rough,] the goddess murmured,[but I promise you, I am with you, my daughter , and my Balgair will be as well.]

Heather could have sworn she heard Ananke sigh, the sound ancient and tender.

[I would like nothing more than to snap my fingers and make your life better, but I'd upset Mother and Des if I did that.]

A faint, rueful humor glimmered in her tone.

[I'm trying to be a good girl, but it's hard sometimes.]

Heather blinked, the corners of her mouth almost lifting in disbelief.

[If you have faith in me, I will provide you with a new family , but that won't happen if you give up on my Balgair.]

Ananke's voice softened until it felt like a whisper shared between heartbeats.

[Balgair won't fail. He's got many people who will be depending upon him, and you'll be the one providing his family with balance.]

The word *family* caught Heather off guard, stirring a deep ache of memory, laughter lost, love broken. She lowered her head and wept quietly, not from despair, but from something gentler.

[It's okay to be afraid,] Ananke breathed into her ear.[Know that my Balgair will move mountains to get you back.]

Heather exhaled, the fear draining from her like smoke. Somewhere beyond the walls, she thought she heard the faint echo of a horn, the same war horn that had called her protector to arms.

In that moment, wrapped in rosemary and the scent of hope, she believed.

Balgair waited another half-hour for the assassin to give up, his patience fraying thread by thread. When it became clear that Yarsmith was not quitting, if anything, the man was hunting him with renewed purpose, Balgair grumbled and rose to his feet.

"Well, for better or worse, I can't wait anymore," he muttered, the words half growl, half prayer. His hand hovered near the latch, breath steady, mind still. He had long ago learned that waiting could be a form of captivity, and Balgair had never worn chains well.

He was just about to open the door
and take the fight to the enemy when a
soft, sensual voice brushed the edge of his
mind, intimate and familiar, though he
had never heard it before.

[Ah, there you are.]

The words shimmered through him,
clear as bells in mist. He turned sharply,
half expecting to find someone standing in
the shadows.

*[If you can wait for a few minutes,
we'll be right there.]*

Balgair blinked and shook his head.
"I must be imagining things." He wasn't
expecting anyone to help him, freedom
meant standing alone, didn't it? Yet the
voice lingered, warm and persuasive, like
sunlight through a narrow window.

269

Down the street, the enchantress shivered as she brushed against the warrior's vibrant prana, an ocean current of will that nearly swept her mind away. "I found him," she whispered, glaring at Brandyn as she rubbed at the goosebumps along her arms. "You didn't tell me that he was so..." Her breath caught, searching for language wide enough to hold what she'd felt. "You didn't tell me he was a true man."

The Tavern master merely commented, "I told you that he was a Captain of the Black Swans." He shook his head. "If you have never met one, then, well, you are in for a surprise."

The enchantress leaned against the thief-taker for balance, drawing in the steadiness of his heartbeat as if to anchor herself. "Oh, I've already been surprised."

Her lips curved, teasing. "If I weren't bound to you, *mo chridhe,* I'd be kneeling at his feet."

The thief-taker chuckled, his voice roughened by affection. "Then aren't I the lucky one? I've got something he can't take." He pulled her close and kissed her cheek, simple as breath.

She fluttered her eyes, giggling softly. "I do love you, you big lout," she confessed, unguarded as a child. "From this world to the next."

For a moment, the air around them seemed to loosen, their laughter dispersing the tension like fog burning off the sea. Saorsa: freedom in its quietest form.

Brandyn gave the two their moment, then started down the street. "Let's go. We've got work to do."

Partway down the alley, the enchantress stopped, eyes bright. "By Nan Diahan, he's an impatient man."

"Whatcha mean?" the thief-taker asked as his bhanna slipped into mind-speech with the captain they were out to save.

"He's very closed-minded and thinks he's imagining my voice," she murmured, glancing toward Brandyn. "What can I tell him to prove that we're on his side?"

The ex-lieutenant sighed. "Tell him I said to keep his shield close and watch his back. That should do it."

She relayed the message, then smiled faintly. "He still doesn't believe me, but he said he'll stay put for now." Relief washed through her. "By Nan Diathan, he's strong." She trembled under the weight of his prana, whispering, "How do women handle men like him?"

The thief-taker's expression softened. "They don't. They surrender completely." He slipped an arm around her shoulders, not as possession, but as recognition. "Do you know where he is?"

"Vaguely," she admitted. "He's not far down the first hall."

Brandyn nodded, steady as bedrock. "If you need to, you can stay outside. I don't want you to lose yourself , nor would he."

"I'll be fine," the enchantress answered, drawing a slow breath. "I just need to break my connection with him." She closed her eyes, centering herself until the line between them softened and released. When she opened her eyes again, she smiled faintly. "His bonds are incredibly lucky."

The Tavern master chuckled low. "You know, I'm starting to think the same thing."

Arien looked from her master to Brandyn, then to the others. "Are all Black Swans that mentally strong?" The question carried awe, not fear. If such men embodied will without tyranny, perhaps there was hope for them all.

Brandyn shrugged. "Not many that I know of. It seems to be a prerequisite to move beyond Captain, to be mentally, physically, and spiritually strong." He paused, gaze distant. "I don't remember my last captain being that strong."

"Is that why you never made Captain?" Arien asked, immediately regretting it when Brandyn's expression darkened. "I'm sorry. I was just curious."

"Don't worry about it," he said after a moment. "But yes. For some reason, I couldn't break through that thin barrier that would grant me a little extra power to make it." His smile turned wistful. "At least I'm in good company."

Ben snorted. "Speak for yourself. I could have made captain; I just didn't want the extra work."

Their laughter rang through the alley, weary, warm, alive. The air lightened again, a reminder that even in the shadow of battle, freedom was not merely survival, but choice: to love, to laugh, to serve, to stand unbound before what comes next.

Chapter Seven

The Call Heard in Darkness

"Gah," the thief-taker muttered as the party crept down the alley, his voice thick with disgust. "Aren't buildings required to have entrances that aren't set in shit-strewn alleys?" He shook his left foot, trying to scrape something foul from the bottom of his boot.

"You don't hear me complaining, love. I'm not wearing boots like you are," Arien whispered, wrinkling her nose. "My slippers are done for. When we get inside, I'm going to have to get rid of them."

The bald man winced, a pang of guilt flickering behind his rough exterior. "I'm sorry, *mo chridhe.* I never imagined we'd be walking through filth."

She patted his arm with quiet affection, her touch grounding them both. The air smelled of damp rot and old sin, freedom's shadowed face. She glanced up at Brandyn, who wore the look of a man at war with his surroundings.

"Yes, city regulations require a front and a rear entrance," Brandyn said, his tone clipped and bitter. "But these criminals obviously thought having two entrances was a bad idea, so they closed off the front." His voice hardened. "That's what the mayor and city inspector should have checked on."

Decay and disorder offended him; a man who had lived by discipline found no liberty in lawlessness.

"I'm sorry to say it doesn't get any better, Lieu," a voice called softly from ahead. Instantly, hands went to weapons, eyes sweeping the shadows. The alley breathed around them, rank, silent, waiting.

"You guys make too much noise," the man complained as he stepped from the dark, his grin cutting through the tension. "Four men and a slave girl trying to sneak down an alley." He shook his head, almost amused. "Could be worse. You could have brought the guard with you."

Brandyn leaned forward, lowering his axe into a ready stance. His eyes narrowed, then softened. "Enrique?"

The cloaked figure nodded and came closer, moving with the fluid grace of a predator that chose mercy. "Yes, sir. I heard the call."

He gave a half-bow, quick and easy. "Ben, Methak, the beautiful Arien, and Scarface." He inclined his head to each. "It's been a while, hasn't it?"

Farank chuckled, recognizing the familiar arrogance. "Riq, what brings you here? This doesn't seem like your normal venue."

The Padfoot smirked. "It isn't the main avenue, but here I am." He turned back to Brandyn. "Would you like a report, sir?"

Brandyn nodded. "Yes, please."

Enrique, Riq to those who'd earned his trust, had always been more spirit than soldier, a man who'd slipped through chains life tried to throw on him.

No one was sure if it was talent or the instincts of a reformed thief, but he moved with the kind of ease that made freedom look effortless.

"The lovely deathtrap before you," he began, gesturing toward the crooked building ahead, "was once two decent housing apartments. Then the silver keys took over, merged them into one big cesspit with one crappy entrance." His hand pointed to the solitary door like an accusation. "About two hundred poor souls are packed inside that lovely deathtrap , and it appears your Captain's already joined them."

The ranger frowned. "What gives you that idea?"

Riq chuckled. "The Clarion Call. That and the dead body outside the door." He gestured to the corpse lying just beyond the alley's mouth, Balgair's earlier work. "This Captain is either very brave or very—" he coughed lightly, "stupid. Forgive me, but it's true. He invaded a deathtrap alone, without backup."

Brandyn only shrugged, his expression unreadable. "I'm not arguing with you. The call speaks for itself."

He hoped the man was still alive, not for the mission's sake, but because the world needed men who still dared to act free.

Methak glanced toward the main street. "Why aren't the guard headed this way? They had to hear the call, right?"

"I'm sure they did," Ben replied. "But they'll need time to suit up and march over. I just hope we can get in and out before they arrive. Once they show, finding either your captain or Heather will be impossible."

Brandyn nodded grimly. "It'll be a disaster, that's for sure." He studied the building, the dead windows, the warped frame, the heavy silence behind the walls. Freedom and captivity shared the same shape here. "Any suggestions, Riq?"

The thief's grin widened as he moved toward the door. "Follow me, stay close, and don't start anything." His eyes caught the splintered hole where a blade had pierced the wood. "Your friend's strong, that's a solid door, and he drove a sword through it."

He eased the door open, peering into the darkness. "It's clear."

Brandyn turned to Arien. "Which way?"

The enchantress paused, her gaze unfocused, her senses reaching out like tendrils of light. She looked right, then left, and finally pointed down the left corridor. "He's down there, somewhere," she said softly.

Brandyn nodded and gestured to Riq, who gathered his cloak and slipped into shadow. The others followed, Brandyn in front, Arien a step behind, the ranger and archer hugging the walls, Farank covering the rear.

At each door, Riq glanced back to Arien. When she shook her head, they moved on. When she finally nodded, he passed the door, ensuring no one lurked behind them.

Brandyn stepped forward, his knuckles rapping three times, pausing, then two more. The sound was almost ceremonial, the rhythm of trust. "We're here, Captain."

The door opened a crack, light spilling into the dim room. Balgair's eyes narrowed as he saw Brandyn's silhouette framed against the corridor's gloom. For a heartbeat, he hesitated, pride and relief warring behind his steady expression, then stepped back and let them enter.

"I'd offer you something to drink, but I wasn't expecting guests." He tried to make light of it, the words an armor of humor over fatigue.

Brandyn didn't return the smile. His gaze, sharp and familiar, spoke of old discipline and deeper concern. "You had me worried, Captain." He placed a firm hand on Balgair's shoulder, not a gesture of command, but of brotherhood reclaimed.

Balgair returned it. "As much as it hurts me to admit it, I'm glad you're here." His voice carried the weight of unspoken lessons.

"I didn't expect this witch to have the help she does. I thought it would be a cakewalk."

Farank shook his head. "If you were facing anyone other than Brigid and the silver keys, you'd be right. But they've taken this building over and treated the residents better than the original owners did. They've turned it into a fortress strong enough to hold off the guard." He tilted his head, listening to distant footsteps. "These people will die before they let the keys be arrested or killed."

Balgair listened, the lines of command in his face softening. "I can see that now." He looked to Brandyn. "Did all of you hear the clarion call?"

"Yes," Methak answered for them all. "As well as saw Mixcoatl's mist on the way." His gaze lingered on Balgair. "Are you worth the risk we are taking?"

Before the captain could reply, the enchantress gasped, her body trembling as Balgair's prana pressed against her like a rising tide. "Oh, he's well worth it," she whimpered as her knees weakened. "You don't know what you are doing to me."

Her voice broke between awe and irritation. "Can you tamp that strength down a bit? I'm having trouble thinking straight."

Balgair exhaled slowly, the air thick with energy and restraint. As he willed his spirit to stillness, the room seemed to ease with him.

When she breathed again, it came as relief. "Oh, thank you. That makes it easier to move." She half-raised her hand in greeting. "My name is Arien; this is my bond master Farank."

Balgair inclined his head. "I wish I had met you under better circumstances." Then, turning to Brandyn, "How is Lucy?"

"She'll be fine," Brandyn said, his tone clipped but reassuring. "Do you know where Heather is being kept?"

"One resident said she would be in the basement," Balgair replied, "where the witch resides."

The ranger's eyes swept over the gouges in the captain's armor. "I see you've already had a run-in with Yarsmith."

"Yes, and his three friends," Balgair said, almost ruefully. "When he realized I could beat him, he summoned two crossbowmen and a silent man with a *pic de' corbin.*"

He bowed his head. "I'm glad you answered the call. If you hadn't, I'd still have gone after Heather , and I think both of us would be dead."

The archer's brow lifted. "Brandyn says you're a chain-maker. Have you bonded with Heather yet?"

"No, I haven't bonded with her yet," Balgair answered quietly. "Now I don't know if she will want to bond with me."

His honesty stilled the air. Methak regarded him anew, respect rising where judgment had been. "From what Brandyn said, she spent the evening with you and didn't run away." At Balgair's nod, Methak's tone softened. "You are the first man she's allowed near her since her parents died and Brutus raped her."

At that, Balgair's composure broke. "May his soul be cast off the wheel," he growled. "That cur is lucky I can only kill him once."

The words burned through the room, hot with fury and pain , the kind of rage born not from vengeance, but from violated freedom.

Brandyn waited, patient as a tide. When Balgair's fury ebbed into silence, he spoke evenly. "Are you sure you're a Captain?"

Balgair blinked. "What?"

"For a professional soldier, you're an *amadan fuilteach*."

Balgair opened his mouth to argue, but Brandyn cut him off. "With all due respect, I suggest you shut the *Ifrinn* up and listen, sir."

His tone held no malice, only the iron steadiness of truth. "Did you scout out the place before you stormed in? Did you talk to the locals and get information about who owned the place? Did you plan and enlist like-minded people to help you?"

Each question struck like hammer blows, breaking apart pride until only self-knowledge remained.

Balgair's silence was long and raw. "No, I didn't." His voice was low. "I've yelled at other soldiers for doing what I did." He drew a breath and released it slowly, as if exhaling the last of his arrogance.

"And rightly so, I'm sure," Ben muttered. "You do know that you could have gone to the Guard and gotten help, right?"

Balgair flinched.

"You're a Black Swan," Ben continued. "Ifrinn, I don't know any guardsman who wouldn't have dropped what he was doing to help you out."

Shame and clarity warred within him, but beneath both was a flicker of release, the moment when a chain of pride quietly falls away.

"I didn't even think about the guard," he admitted, shaking his head. "I wouldn't blame you if you dragged me out of here and threw me into the stockade."

"Yeah, well, there's always that option," Farank grumbled, half serious.

Arien, still pale but smiling, broke the tension. "But we won't do that. If we did that, we'd have to leave Heather in their hands, and I don't want to do that."

Her words settled over them like a benediction. Freedom, she reminded them, wasn't vengeance or pride, it was compassion, even in the filth of a fortress built on fear.

The air inside the narrow room had settled, that rare, crystalline stillness that comes when resolve replaces fear. Balgair stood beside Brandyn, the weariness of guilt behind him now, replaced by something quieter: readiness.

Brandyn grunted his agreement and spoke again. "It's time to introduce you to my little crew." He pointed to the Thief-taker and the Enchantress. "This is Farank and his bond, Arien."

When the two nodded, he gestured toward the cloaked man listening at the door. "Our sneaky friend is Enrique. The archer is Methak, and the ranger is Ben," he added, nodding toward the men by the window.

Balgair's gaze moved over them, studying each face, each weapon, each subtle sign of experience and intent. "It's an honor," he said, meaning it. The old habit of assessing others in silence still lingered, but for the first time in a long while, it was joined by respect instead of suspicion.

Brandyn chuckled softly, hearing that shift in his tone. "Would the Captain be willing to take some advice from an old Lieutenant?"

Balgair's answer came without hesitation, a small but potent act of humility. When he nodded, the Tavern Master outlined his plan with calm assurance. "Enrique should scout ahead and see if there's a way around Yarsmith and his cronies. You and I should go next because we've got the armor and weapons to stand up to Yarsmith and his polearm-wielding friend." He looked over at Ben and Methak. "The ranger and archer come next to see if they can deter the crossbowmen, and Arien will use her sorcery from cover and watch our backs."

As Brandyn spoke, a sense of balance settled over the group, each person finding their place in the rhythm of danger, each role woven into the next like threads in a single braid.

"That's a good call, Lieutenant," Balgair acknowledged. His voice carried gratitude wrapped in steel. "I was hesitant to involve anyone else in my problem, but since you've all volunteered, I won't tell you how to do your jobs."

He paused as the corners of their mouths lifted, quiet smiles between comrades who understood the same risk. "I want you all to be very careful and not die on my account."

The archer grunted, "I owe that mageling a knock upside the head. So don't think about it."

"If that's all," the thief whispered, "I'll see if I can get around them."

He opened the door and peered down the hall. The dim light cut across his features, a half-shadowed grin, all confidence and mischief. "I may have to go up one level and come down behind them."

At Balgair's nod, Enrique slipped through the door, a whisper of fabric and breath, and was gone, freedom incarnate, moving unseen through narrow space.

"How long should we wait?" Balgair asked after a moment, his instinct for command tempered now by patience. "For that matter, are Yarsmith and his men still out there?"

"Yes, they are still there," Arien murmured, her voice dreamlike as she leaned against Farank. "Hmmm. They are wondering where you went." A soft hum escaped her lips, a sound between thought and melody. "Rique decided to go up a level. He's about halfway up to the third-story window."

She opened her eyes, pupils faintly luminescent. "Do we want to wait for him to get behind them, or do we want to brave the hallway?"

"Let's wait for him to get where he's going," Balgair decided, his tone calm but resolute. "As far as I know, we aren't in any big hurry."

Arien nodded, continuing to trace the thief's progress with her mind's eye. Her gift flowed through her lightly now, no longer burdened by Balgair's overwhelming prana, but harmonized with it. "He's entered through a window and is talking to the woman inside."

A faint blush rose to her cheeks. "He's sweet-talking his way out of her apartment," she mumbled. Then, after a moment's pause, she chuckled. "So far, she's agreed not to call for help, but she will want something from him."

Ben nudged Methak, whispering a quick comment that made the archer stifle a laugh. Brandyn and Farank shared a knowing glance while Arien's blush deepened into a crimson that even the candlelight could not hide.

Balgair allowed himself a half-smile, the tension in his shoulders easing. "I'm sure she will," he said, leaving the rest unspoken, to the enchantress's quiet gratitude.

The laughter that followed was soft and brief, but it filled the small room with warmth, the laughter of those who had seen enough of death to treasure every heartbeat of reprieve.

Outside, the city's air stirred, cold, fetid, and restless, but within those walls, something sacred took hold: not courage born of rage, but calm born of trust.

For the first time since he'd entered this forsaken place, Balgair felt free, not because he stood apart, but because he finally stood *with* them.

Chapter Eight

The Summoning of the Dark Weaver

The chamber reeked of damp stone and burnt incense, the scent of blood still lingering beneath it, heavy, metallic, inescapable. Shadows clung to every seam of the room, like ink pooling where the world refused to look.

Heather sat in the circle's half-light, her heart drumming a rhythm between courage and despair. The runes beneath her pulsed with dull, unnatural color, as though the floor itself breathed. She swallowed hard, gathering what strength she could, and reached out with her mind.

[Is he still coming to get me?]

Her thoughts carried through the veil, fragile but resolute, a whispered plea flung into eternity.

Ananke did not answer at once. The silence stretched thin as frost on glass, a silence that felt *too long*, even for a goddess.

[Yes, he is,] came the eventual reply, gentle as moonlight,[and he's not alone. It seems he's found some help.]

Relief flickered through Heather, quickly chased by disbelief.

[Who did he find?] she asked, surprised. [There aren't that many people who would even speak to me after what happened.]

The goddess hesitated again, not from reluctance, but from the weight of what must be said. When Ananke spoke, her voice carried an echo of sorrow.

[There is that man that was behind the bar, a ranger with a Chamelo-cloak, an archer with a very impressive longbow, a thief with a stealth cloak, a man I don't know, and a bonded enchantress.]

Heather blinked, dazed. *Brandyn.* Of course he'd come. He and Balgair had shared that rare brotherhood born only from men who had bled together in wars past.

Still, shame crept over her like a chill as she thought of Ben and Methak how she had scorned their kindness, turned away their help. And yet they had come. They had all come.

Only the names she did not know the thief, the stranger, the enchantress unsettled her. *Why would anyone else risk their lives for me?*

Her thoughts broke as Brigid's sing-song voice cut through the gloom.

"Almost done, little sacrifice."

The witch's words slithered through the air, playful and cruel. Her hands moved with maddening precision over the carved runes, fingertips tracing symbols older than language itself.

Heather's skin prickled; cold sweat gathered at her temples. Fear had weight here, it pressed on her shoulders, whispered in her ears.

"There, there," Brigid crooned, her tone mockingly tender. "Soon, it'll be over, and you won't have to worry about anything anymore."

The witch's eyes gleamed with an unholy light as she began to chant. Each word trembled with the power of the *Draoidheacd*, the ancient sorcery that had once bound gods and unmade kings.

"Come to me, great one. Come to me, Ancient One. Come to me, Chaos Bringer. Come to me, dark bringer."

Her voice echoed in rhythmic waves, a tide of invocation that made the walls quiver.

"Come to me, unbinder. Come to me, dreamless one. Come to me, Sleepless one. Come to me, undoer of life. Come to me, Shadow Lord."

The runes flared one after another, each feeding the next, a chain of light becoming shadow, of power becoming hunger. A vortex bloomed at the circle's center, not as a flame or portal, but as *absence itself.* It drew breath from the room, from the torches, from Heather's lungs.

The light died slowly, like a dying star collapsing into silence.

Heather cracked her eyes open, just long enough to see the dark spiral eating its own edges. Shadows grew thicker, coiling around her ankles, licking up the air until even memory of light seemed to vanish.

Her heart began to race.

[I can't do this. Please stay with me, Milady.]

Her prayer came not as command, but confession.

The darkness deepened in answer, a presence vast and watching, a silence that did not care.

She didn't think it could get any darker, but somehow it did. The world folded in on itself until there was only breath and heartbeat, and even those were slipping away.

Then came the moment all souls know when faced with the divine: the point where terror outpaces will.

Heather's body failed her before her faith did.

She exhaled one small, broken breath, and the world fell away. She fainted, not from weakness, but because no mortal heart could hold that much fear and still remain whole.

And as her consciousness ebbed, Ananke's final whisper brushed her fading thoughts, neither command nor comfort, only truth:

[Hold fast, child. Even the dark must dream.]

Balgair froze. The air had changed, subtly at first, like the moment before lightning splits the sky, when the world seems to hold its breath. Then, the pressure built until even his armor felt heavier.

If he had to describe it, it would be as if something *bigger and meaner than them* had turned its gaze their way, a beast too vast to see, only to feel, stalking them from the folds of the unseen.

He wasn't alone in sensing it. Behind him, Arien faltered mid-step. Her lips tightened, and she closed her eyes, as though trying to shut out a sound too high or deep for mortal hearing. The enchantress pressed a hand against the wall, her brow furrowed.

"Uck," she uttered, shuddering as though something cold had brushed her mind. She withdrew her senses from what lay below. "We're almost out of time. Brigid is trying to open a portal to the outer dark."

Balgair's voice was rough, uncertain. "The Outer Dark? You mean, the outer dark where the Sleepless Ones lie?"

"The very one," Arien affirmed grimly. "We need to get going. If she succeeds and frees one of the ancient ones, we will have a harder time with this." Her eyes lifted, distant for a heartbeat. "Rique is at the stairs and starting down."

The hallway seemed to tilt around them. The light from the lanterns dimmed, though the flames did not shrink. A shadow of pressure moved through the air, not a wind, not a sound, but a *presence*, like a mountain bending over them to listen.

And below, the witch's voice answered that pressure.

"Oh yes, come to me, Dark One. Come to me, Chaos Bringer. Come to me, creeping one."Brigid's chant filled the chamber like black water seeping through cracks. Her fingers trembled with fervor as she drew upon the *Draoidheacd*, the ancient power that fed on sacrifice. "I've got your sacrifice here."

The runes blazed, each one bleeding light until the circle burned white, then red, then black. For a heartbeat, Brigid thought she had failed, and in that heartbeat, the silence cracked.

The portal stabilized.

From within the vortex, something moved, slow and deliberate, like an idea becoming flesh. Shadows coiled inward, drawn as if by gravity, and then erupted into a single, shrouded form.

The air went thin. The god *breathed.*

It was not a sound, but the absence of it, one single long inhalation, drawn from every corner of the room, as though the chamber itself emptied its lungs. The figure held that stolen breath for a long, dreadful moment before exhaling it back as cold vapor that smelled of iron and endings.

Two red eyes opened beneath the cowl. They did not glow so much as they revealed , cutting through shadow, finding Brigid first, then turning toward the unconscious blond lying in the circle.

[You have done well, my daughter,]

The voice was not spoken; it resonated *through* her, ancient, intimate, terrible.

Each word filled her skull like molten metal, searing devotion into her bones.

The ancient one stepped forward with the slow grace of something that had never needed to hurry. Each movement displaced the world, a ripple in reality's weave.

[You will be well rewarded.]

The words were promise and hunger intertwined.

Brigid shuddered in ecstasy as his dark *prana* slid over her like smoke. It caressed her spirit the way a lover might trace a spine, gentle, claiming, inescapable. Visions flooded her mind: palaces of shadow, power unbound, pleasures without end. Her breath caught in a moan she could not suppress.

"Yes, Maighstir," she crooned softly, trembling.

The black-robed god regarded her in silence, and the room seemed to bow inward, as though gravity itself had decided who now ruled.

"If she's trying to summon an ancient one, we've got to hurry," Arien stated.

Balgair glanced at Brandyn and gave a single nod. His jaw was tight, his eyes sharp beneath the dim, flickering lantern light. He hefted his shield, the metal catching what little glow remained, and murmured a prayer so quiet it barely left his lips. It was not a plea for victory, but for strength, for the gods to remember their own.

When Farank opened the door, a breath of stagnant air met them. It smelled of stone, old iron, and something else, something *waiting*. Balgair stepped into the hallway first, his boots whispering over the dust. The others followed.

He waited until Brandyn joined him, and together, both men angled their shields forward, not in defiance, but in reverence. The two old warriors moved as one, advancing down the corridor with the quiet, measured rhythm of men who had walked through death before and found it wanting.

Ten heartbeats later, Methak and Ben emerged, their boots making almost no sound. They nocked arrows in unison, slipping into the shadows like hunters of the unseen.

Another ten seconds passed before Farank and Arien entered, the thief-taker glancing about while the enchantress half-closed her eyes, listening to something the others could not hear.

She shivered, her skin paling. The Thief-taker caught the tremor and frowned.

"It's nothing, *cor meum,*" she said with a forced smile. Her voice was soft, but the lie was fragile. "The ancient one is slowly manifesting." She drew a deep breath, centering herself against the oppressive pull beneath their feet. "If it weren't for him," she gestured toward Balgair, "the darkness would subsume us all. Only Balgair's prana is protecting us."

Her body trembled again, though this time not from fear alone. "I underestimated how strong he is, you know."

The thief-taker grunted, his tone warm despite the weight in the air. "You keep saying that, and if I were a lesser man, I'd feel jealous."

The enchantress giggled softly, the sound like a fragile bell in the void. "You are anything but lesser, *cor meum.*" Her gaze drifted down the hall, where she could *feel* Balgair's presence, steady, radiant, vast. His prana pulsed like a heartbeat in the dark. "I hope it's going to be enough."

"This is damned odd," Balgair muttered, his voice low and wary, as they advanced another twenty paces.

The corridor seemed longer than it should have been, stretching like a dream refusing to end. "Where did they go? Surely they know I didn't run out on them."

"Peace, brother," Brandyn murmured, his tone calm and grounding. "They may have withdrawn to cover the stairs leading up and down."

"That's what worries me," Balgair admitted quietly, though he didn't voice his deeper fear, that Heather was somewhere below, alone in the dark.

He reached out with his thoughts. [*Milady, how is Heather?*]

The silence that followed was wrong. Heavy. Dead.

When Ananke didn't answer, Balgair frowned. He stopped mid-step, raising his free hand for quiet. His eyes closed, his mind reaching out again. [*Milady Ananke, where are you?*]

Nothing. Not even the echo of her presence.

"What's wrong?" Brandyn asked, noting the shift in his friend's expression.

The mercenary opened his eyes slowly, his face pale beneath the flickering torchlight. "Something happened to Ananke," he said. "I can't hear her anymore."

The ex-soldier blinked, his voice rough. "What in the seven levels of Ifrinn can mute a goddess?"

"I don't know," Balgair admitted. "Why don't you try and see if you can talk to Huitzilopochtli? He is your god, right?"

"Yep." Brandyn's answer was steady, but when he tried, his brow furrowed. The silence that met him was vast, colder than any battlefield silence. He lowered his head, eyes wide. "What's going on here?"

When Balgair only shrugged helplessly, Brandyn turned to Ben and Methak. "Can you sense Mixcoatl at all?"

The ranger and the archer exchanged a look. They tried, closing their eyes, focusing as they had a hundred times before, but when nothing came, the air seemed to tighten around them.

"He's never failed to answer us," the ranger whispered, disbelief threading through the awe in his voice.

Methak's hand tightened on his bow. "What are we up against?" he asked, the question trembling between them like a prayer that had forgotten how to find heaven.

In the basement, the air had grown thick , a quiet that was not silence but the holding of breath before creation remembers itself. The shadows pulsed faintly, as if the stone walls themselves waited for command.

The Ancient One stood motionless within the circle, his shape only half-defined, as though the darkness refused to release him entirely. His cowl hid everything but the gleam of two faint embers, eyes that burned without light, without warmth.

He bent over the unconscious blond, his presence folding around her like nightfall. His hand lifted, long and deliberate, until it hovered a finger's width above her chest. A low hum shuddered through the air, a denial not from her, but from something *within* her.

The god's hand halted, his gaze unreadable beneath the hood. He turned, the motion smooth as water.

[Why do you bring me a sacrifice that I cannot use?]

Outside the circle, Brigid paled, her confidence cracking like porcelain. "I don't... What do you mean you can't use her?" Her voice trembled; fear warred with anger, the same anger she always turned upon herself.

The Ancient One tilted his head, and the air cooled further.

[No, her physical injuries have no impact on her soul, and it's her soul I can't use.]

He leaned closer to the still woman, his shadow spilling like oil across the floor.

[Where did you get her?]

"We took her from a bar. Nobody will miss her," Brigid said quickly, defensively. "Does that make a difference?"

[No, it doesn't.]

He traced a sigil in the air above Heather. The rune burned white for an instant, then turned gold and inverted. The god's voice deepened, almost reverent.

[Apparently, this woman is under the protection of Ananke.]

He rose to his full height, the circle's light bending away from him.

Brigid's breath caught. "Does this mean that I failed?"

[No, you didn't fail.]

He took a step forward, to the very edge of the circle. The shadows recoiled from his feet.

[I am free from the prison my father put me in.]

He pointed once toward Heather's prone form.

[She was just a bonus. As soon as you release me from this circle, I will give you everything that you asked for.]

Brigid's heartbeat thundered in her ears. "Everything? Even...?"

The robed head inclined.

"Everything. You will have the power you wish, and Mac Draoidheacd will have to admit that you have it."

Temptation moved through her like a tide. She stared at the circle, at the small gap between salvation and damnation. Then, very gently, she extended her foot and scuffed the line.

Light bled away.

She fell to her knees, trembling. "Welcome to Crann Na Beatha, Maighstir."

[It is good to be home, daughter,]

he said, resting one hand upon her bowed head. The touch was deceptively light, and yet every nerve in her body burned with rapture.

[You have questions, don't you?]

Brigid nodded, breathless.

[Could you remove Ananke's protection?]

[I can, but I won't.]

His fingers slipped through her hair; her shiver was almost worship.

[Were I to remove her protection, the guardian and the dreamer would know. I am not ready to face them yet.]

Confusion clouded her eyes. "I don't understand. Why aren't you mad?"

The Ancient One looked down at her as though seeing a child.

[You had no way of knowing she was protected. My anger over that would be a waste of time and energy.]

The calm certainty in his tone unmade her fear.

[As for the other, I must gather followers before I face my family again.]

His words were steady, patient, and cold, the resolve of something that had survived eternity in chains.

[Come, we have work to do.]

"As you wish, Ancient One." She rose, unsteady. "What are we going to do with her?"

[Nothing. We will leave her here in the dark.]

He turned his gaze upward, the air trembling under it.

[What would you have me do to your uninvited guests?]

Brigid frowned. "Can you kill them?"

[I could, but that would alert the others.]

Her concern shifted from vengeance to loyalty. "Can you save my followers?"

[I can, but they need to come quickly before they are engaged in battle.]

He returned to the dark vortex, his gestures slow, deliberate, reshaping it like a craftsman shaping metal.

Brigid stared for a long moment, then reached out with her mind.

[The Ancient One is free. He wants you to avoid combat and get down here.]

Yarsmith's thought came back sharp.

[Why? We can beat them.]

Brigid's eyes flicked toward the cowl. It shifted faintly from side to side.

[He says our lady of chains, the great dreamer, and the guardian protect them. He, I know it's going to, just get down here, Indigo. I don't want to go without you.]

A pause, then grudging acceptance.

[Understood, we'll be down in a minute. They are attempting to trap us.]

She could picture his expression perfectly: that tight-lipped disapproval that was never quite anger. He never *did* show anger.

From the circle's heart came a low chuckle, not cruel, not kind. Simply amused.

Brigid turned toward the sound. "Maighstir, my men say that the intruders are trying to trap them. Can you help them get away?"

She bowed her head as she spoke. Humility came easily now.

[If you wish it, I can do so, but I will require something in return.]

Her pulse quickened. What could an ancient god possibly want for such a small favor?

He read the thought as she formed it. The cowl tilted slightly, as though enjoying her internal struggle. Her imagination ran wild, servitude, sacrifice, the giving of flesh or the taking of another's life.

And beneath it all, one constant truth: for *him*, for *Indigo*, she would do anything.

[All I need is your undying worship, Brigid Ulsdottir.]

He turned fully toward her, and she felt the pull of eternity in his gaze.

[I want you to be my priestess.]

The words wrapped around her like a crown of shadow. heavy, exquisite, final.

Without hesitation, she dropped to her knees again. "If it pleases you, my maighstir, please save my followers."

The god's lips curved beneath the hood, unseen but felt.

"It shall be done."

The darkness answered him like a choir.

The air convulsed as inky tendrils gathered in the basement, weaving through shadow and breath until they thickened into substance. They coiled once, like serpents preparing to strike, then shot upward, through cracks and stairwells, through the veins of the dying house.

In a heartbeat, the tendrils burst through the door above, circling the stairwell in a widening gyre before collapsing upon themselves. They wrapped around Yarsmith and his men like strands of midnight silk, and the world blinked.

Between one breath and the next, they were *gone* from the hallway and *there* in the basement, deposited soundlessly at the bottom of the stairs. The scent of burnt iron and cold stone greeted them.

The assassin was the first to move. Silent as always, Yarsmith took in the scene: Brigid kneeling at the feet of a black-robed figure, her hands trembling, her head bowed. The runes that had once trapped the god flickered dimly, one line erased, one boundary broken.

He raised a hand, signaling for his men to remain. The gesture was habit, unnecessary, but it gave him time to steady his pulse.

Then he crossed the chamber, each step soft and measured, his boots whispering across the faded sigils.

When he reached the figure, he knelt, lowering his eyes to the floor as reverence and curiosity warred within him.

"Great one," he whispered, the words more exhale than speech.

Seeing their leader kneel, the others followed , one by one, until the room seemed to tilt beneath the weight of collective submission.

As their praise rose like smoke, the Ancient One straightened. The shadows clung to him as though unwilling to part. The air itself bent, humming faintly as their faith strengthened him, knitting substance to spirit.

[You may rise.]

The assassin obeyed, standing slowly, meeting the unseen gaze beneath the cowl.

[You have questions. Ask them.]

Yarsmith's eyes flicked to Brigid, still kneeling, head bowed, then returned to the god. "Why did you have us pull back?"

The Ancient One turned toward the portal, his movements deliberate, almost lazy. The voice that followed was a calm so complete it bordered on indifference.

[I dare not draw the attention of the others, and Ananke cherishes the man you were squaring off against, while one of the others is under the Dreamer's gaze.]

[The time is not right for the others to know I am here.]

He extended one long arm toward the swirling ink of the portal, reshaping it with gestures that made the air quiver.

[You can, of course, do what you wish. However,] he gestured toward Brigid, **[my priestess and I are going to meet with others who follow me.]**

The assassin studied him for a moment, then inclined his head. "**If you allow it, we will go with you.**"

[It is of no consequence to me.]

The god stepped toward the portal.

[If we wish to leave, it must be now.]

He pointed to Brigid.

[You lead the way, then your cohort, then the Assassin, then me.]

"Yes, Maighstir," Brigid breathed. The words no longer trembled; they *rang*. She rose gracefully, the motion fluid, reverent, the movement of a priestess anointed not by light, but by the weight of her own surrender. She took a long breath and stepped into the darkness.

"What about her?" one of the crossbowmen asked, glancing toward Heather's still form, pale against the stone.

[Leave her,] the god said, his voice low and final. **[Ananke protects her.]**

"It's a shame we can't take her with us," the man murmured as he fell into line.

Yarsmith placed a steadying hand on his shoulder. "We'll find you another doxy when we get to wherever he's leading us."

And with that, they followed , first Brigid, then her faithful, then the assassin, and finally the god.

One by one, they stepped into the living darkness, and the portal devoured their silhouettes.

The sound of their departure was not thunder or wind, it was silence, deep and resonant, as if the world itself had swallowed a breath it could never release.

Only Heather remained, unconscious in the dim, her golden hair spread across the floor like the last memory of dawn. Around her, the sigils shimmered weakly, still alive, still holding.

Far above, unseen, the gods of Saorsa stirred, their divine voices quiet, their attention sharpened. The balance trembled. The first church of the Fallen had been born beneath the earth.

Chapter Nine

The Light Rekindled

The corridor breathed like a throat, narrow, stale, and waiting. Dust hung in the lantern-void, shimmering only when a bolt scraped stone and sang away into darkness. Balgair moved with his shield canted just so, each footfall measuring the distance between courage and caution. Around him, men and vows kept pace.

Balgair and his crew moved down the hall, taking occasional shots at their enemies. Every time they thought they had them cornered, Yarsmith and his cronies managed to escape being captured.

"Where are the stairs down?" Balgair asked as he peeked around a corner, ducking back as a crossbow bolt sailed through the space where his head had been seconds earlier.

Arien's lashes flickered as she listened past walls and footfalls, reading the house like a wounded beast. She lifted a hand, a quick, spare motion that spoke in angles Arien looked up, then made a gesture that could be construed as around the corner, and whispered, "Riq is almost to his set of stairs, if they are in the same place on this level, around the corner and twenty feet down the hall."

"That twenty feet might as well be a hundred," Ben said as he nocked an arrow and edged his foot around the corner.

He nodded at Balgair, who edged the shield out to provide some cover for the ranger. As a crossbow bolt pinged off the shield, Ben slid around the corner, took aim at one of the opposition, and released. He was rewarded by the sound of a crossbow hitting the ground. "That's one less weapon to shoot us with," he commented as he ducked back around the corner to avoid another bolt.

The air felt thicker after every shot, as if something below had begun to draw breath.

Methak pulled an arrow from his quiver and nocked it. "Just leaves one more to take out." He nodded to Brandyn, who knelt and stuck his shield out. He frowned when nobody took the bait, then carefully stuck the bow around the corner.

When he dared to stick his head out, he shook his head. "They're gone. Think they've retreated to the stairs?"

Balgair nodded and stepped around the corner, his shield held out and angled up. "Probably, let's get going."

Boots whispered; leather sighed. Brandyn rose with a grunt and fell into the old rhythm at Balgair's shoulder, two soldiers walking an edge together. The others flowed in behind like a shadow with many feet.

Brandyn grunted as he got up and followed Balgair. With the two in front again, the rest fell in behind them and followed them down the hall.

Farank tried a smile where the light refused to."It could be worse," Farank commented, earning a groan from Balgair and Brandyn.

"Now you went and did it," Arien glanced at him. "If it gets bad, it's your fault." The thief-catcher just grinned as if it didn't bother him.

"That's okay," Balgair grinned. "If something goes wrong, we'll stick him out front and use him to block arrows."

"You wouldn't," Farank said, then sucked in a breath. "Would you?" He took a step back and waved in distress.

Brandyn and Ben glanced at Balgair, assessed his behavior, and shook their heads. "You're evil," The barkeep stated.

The Mercenary managed to assume an innocent expression. "Who me? I'll have you know that Milady doesn't think I'm evil."

Methak snorted, "She wouldn't. Our Lady of Chains wouldn't think you were evil even if you enslaved whole cities."

Balgair looked disgusted. "If I did that, she'd kill me." He grumbled, "Enslaving." He shuddered and then quietly marched down the hallway.

The house seemed to narrow with every step, as if the timbers themselves leaned in to listen. Fifteen steps bore them to a new line of fate.

Fifteen steps later, Balgair stopped and looked down the hallway to where Yarsmith and his crew were standing before a doorway.

The assassin looked up and saw Balgair's crew. They saw him at the same time he saw them.

Their stillness felt older than combat, more like two oaths measuring each other.

Balgair stared at the assassin for a moment. "Was it worth it, assassin?" When Yarsmith didn't answer, the Mercenary shook his head, "Was it?"

Yarsmith shrugged, "If he escapes his prison, yes. It was worth it."

"He?" Balgair blinked. "You're trying to release one of the ancients." Yarsmith allowed a ghost of a smile to cross his face. "Do I have to go through you to get Heather back?"

"If our positions were reversed, what would you do?" The assassin asked as he drew his daggers and held them across his chest.

"I don't know," Balgair admitted. "Neither my god nor I would ever hold a person hostage."

"Don't they?" Yarsmith inquired. "What else is the great wheel, other than the ultimate hostage system?"

The words struck like a gloved hand. Somewhere in the depths, the world seemed to hesitate. not from fear, but from listening. Balgair reached inward for Ananke and found only the clean, terrible space where her voice should be. The silence didn't scold; it examined.

Balgair had never given it any thought, and he would have loved to discuss it with Ananke but still couldn't contact her. It must have shown on his face because Yarsmith smirked. "Sucks not being able to talk to your god, doesn't it?"

A thousand thoughts rose like sparks; Balgair stamped them down to ash. The sword sang free, a cold line in warm hands. A thousand thoughts ran through Balgair's mind, but he tamped them down and stepped toward Yarsmith, "I don't need to talk to the gods to take you down." With a determined look, he drew his sword from the sheath and pointed it at the assassin. "Are you ready for round two?"

The house answered before Yarsmith could. The light thinned; the air cooled; the hallway's end unstitched itself and rewove as absence. Before he could attack Yarsmith, the air around the stairway darkened, and an archway of pure darkness formed behind the assassin's crew.

"What the Ifrinn?" Balgair cursed as fingers of darkness reached out of the basement doorway and crept down the hall toward where the assassin and his cohorts were standing. As the inky darkness wrapped around the assassin's crew like a second skin, Yarsmith glanced down, then glanced at Balgiar, before flashing a grin. There was a moment of absolute darkness as the fingers closed around Yarsmith and his men.

The breath left the corridor. Even the wood forgot to creak. "Get ready," Brandyn warned as he watched the inky darkness. "They are ..." he paused, shocked as the darkness lifted slightly, and the assassin and his cohorts were gone. He fixed Balgair with a shocked look, and the mercenary shrugged.

In the Saorsa hush that followed, the company stood within a question vast enough to swallow gods: Were they acting by will, or being moved by a will older than light? The only answer was the echo of their own hearts.

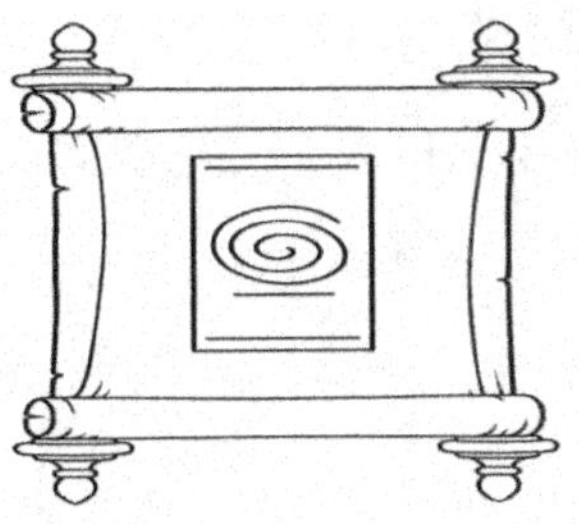

The air felt hollow in the wake of Yarsmith's vanishing. The darkness that had swallowed him now retreated down the corridor like a tide drawing secrets back to sea, leaving behind only the faint ache of something vast having passed through.

"Where did they go?" Ben asked as he lowered his bow so that it rested across his body.

Balgair stared at where the darkness was slowly disappearing, his breath shallow. It was not absence that he saw but *withholding*, as if the shadows still watched from the edges. He took a step forward. "Maybe they ran."

Arien looked over Balgair's shoulder, her brow furrowed as the last of the inky tendrils drew back through the stairwell.

"But why?" she asked, voice half prayer, half disbelief. "Oh my, she released the Ancient One." Her tone carried the weight of a name no mortal should speak aloud. She looked at Balgair, her voice softening. "I hope your Heather is okay."

Balgair met her eyes, the faintest flicker of light in the growing dim. "Me too," he affirmed, his voice lower than before. He took another step toward the stairs.

[Milady, can you hear me? Is Heather okay?]

The plea was swallowed whole by the still air. Not even the faint hum of divine awareness stirred in his mind. That silence, usually comforting, now pressed against him like a tombstone.

"Could something happen to nan Diathan?"

Arien paled at the question. The very thought seemed to steal the strength from her hands. "If something did, we could be seeing the beginning of worldwide chaos." Her whisper trembled. "Nobody wants to face a world without the gods." She looked back toward the fading dark. "What does it feel like to you?"

Balgair stopped. He weighed the silence before answering. "It's almost as if the gods are holding their breaths." The phrase hung between them, vast and fragile. "Almost as if they are waiting for something to happen." He frowned, the sensation gnawing at him. "I've never felt anything like this before."

"Like what, chain-maker?" Brandyn asked, glancing back down the hallway. The old soldier's hands were steady, but his voice betrayed unease. Flesh and blood enemies he could meet with steel; the supernatural always left him cold.

"How can I describe it?" Balgair's words faltered. "It's as if everything is frozen in time. I can't feel Lady Ananke. It's so strange."

The ranger closed his eyes and murmured a prayer. When he opened them again, something in his gaze had changed, like a man who'd just checked a compass and found it spinning. "Mixcoatl isn't saying a word. Whatever this is has got him concerned."

"That's not good," the archer muttered. "When the gods get worried, I usually lie low."

He glanced at Ben, who only shrugged. Other than a few spells, neither relied much on the First Dreamer. Their distance now felt like insulation, and exile.

"Well, that's not going to happen," Methak growled, his tone grounding them all again. "We've still got a woman to save."

In his mind, Heather's name was both promise and penance. He would see her safe, even if another's arms awaited her at the end of the road.

Balgair listened to the voices of his companions, their humor, their courage, their fear, and found in them a fragile comfort. He was about to tell them to move when a voice called from above.

"Hey, what gives?" Rique's head appeared through the doorway, his expression a puzzled frown. "Why is it so quiet here?" He scanned the hall. "Where did the suckers go?"

Balgair could only shrug. "Come on, guys, let's get a move on." And before anyone could stop him, he stepped through the doorway leading down into the basement.

The darkness took him instantly. It wasn't the soft dark of a cellar or the moonless night of the road, it was total, absolute, deliberate. The kind that unmade the idea of light itself. His breath echoed strangely, as though swallowed and released by something vast. He stopped, instinct pressing him back to the wall. "Be careful, it's pitch dark in here."

Their voices answered faintly behind him, reassurance woven through fear. He stretched his left hand out, fingers brushing cold stone, and felt his way downward. For a heartbeat, he thought there was no floor, that he was stepping into eternity, and then his boot found a step. He exhaled, shaky but grateful.

He couldn't help but wonder what had done this. The hallway above had still known the touch of torchlight, but here, even memory struggled. "Arien, any ideas of why it's so dark?" he called over his shoulder.

"No," came the enchantress's reply, faint and distant, as if the dark itself bent sound. "It's unnatural though. If it weren't, there'd be some light." She looked up or tried to. "It's like the light stops at the door."

Balgair nodded, though no one could see it. "I wish we had some light." His voice sounded small, like a wish whispered to a forgotten god.

"I'm trying," Arien said after a pause, frustration bleeding into her tone. "But whatever is doing this is more powerful than I am."

"Then it was an ancient one that they freed," Balgair murmured as he took another step down. If anything, the pitch-black space grew heavier. Before, he'd seen faint shapes, now he couldn't see even the ghost of his own hand.

[My Lady of Chains, I could use some light.]

Nothing answered, not a whisper, not the warmth of presence that usually curled around his thoughts.

Even the Clarion Call, that quiet hum of divine resonance, had gone mute. It was as though the world had stopped breathing.

He hesitated, then, with exaggerated care, found the next step.

"Be careful, Captain. It wouldn't be good to fall," Brandyn warned behind him. The old soldier's voice was rough but steady, a tether in the void. He would never admit it, but the darkness pressed on him too. He'd rather face ten men in daylight than one ghost in this black.

It was loyalty, not courage, that kept him moving, that, and the five souls behind him who followed the Captain's steps into the unknown.

"If I move any slower, a slug could beat me," Balgair retorted, his voice half amusement, half exhaustion. The sound was strange in this lightless place, swallowed, not echoed, as if the air itself disapproved of levity. He wondered why he was treating the tavern master as if they were old friends. Perhaps it was because they were both soldiers, and soldiers understood what it meant to keep moving when the dark pressed too close.

With a shake of his head, he found the next step, his palm sliding along the cold stone. Each block felt older than memory, carved in a time before torches, before speech, when only the gods could see.

It was amazing how much you took light for granted, until it was gone. In the dark, the mind made light a religion. "Arien," he called softly, "isn't there something you can do about this darkness?"

His ears filled instantly with her complaints. "I can't even see my hand in front of my face, and the man wants light. As if I could wave my hands and command it." She stomped her foot, the sound dull and close, like a heartbeat swallowed in fog. "Why, I oughta."

The ranger's voice drifted from behind, teasing to mask his unease. "Well, don't you? Don't you normally wave your hand and say something like *Ignis*?"

Arien's voice sharpened. "If I could see you, I'd show you waving, you idiotic ranger! Of all the stupid things to say." Her tone softened into frustrated muttering. "For your information, I must have something to use as a light source before making it brighter. It could be a candle, a torch, a glimmer from a window, but I can't *create* light if it doesn't already exist. And the absence of light in this stairwell isn't helping."

Her words fell like stones into the suffocating quiet. The darkness pressed closer, feeding on every sound.

Balgair felt it, the way a soldier feels the weight of an unseen arrow. Doubt crept into his thoughts, thick as smoke. The air seemed heavier, as though the world itself were mourning.

He wondered, not for the first time, if his bonds would even miss him should he fall here and vanish. That thought froze him mid-step.

"Hey there," Brandyn muttered, sensing the stillness. "What gives, chain-maker?" He reached forward, his hand brushing armor, and gave Balgair a push that nearly sent him tumbling. "You had better not give up on us, Captain." His voice was a growl—gruff, grounding. He shoved Balgair against the wall, found his shoulder, then his face. "If you give up on me, I'll throw you down the stairs. Shake it off, man."

For a moment, Balgair didn't breathe. The darkness held its breath with him. Then, after an eternity compressed into a heartbeat, he drew in a slow, heavy breath that tasted of stone and despair.

"I'd deserve it," he admitted, the words thick and tired. "I was just thinking about how oppressive this feels."

He exhaled, then inhaled again deliberate, anchoring. "I started wondering if they'd even miss me."

If Brandyn could have seen his eyes, he would have seen them wide with terror—then narrowing, steadying, hardening into tempered steel. "Thank you for helping me, Brandyn."

"As if you're the first to feel fear," the tavern master muttered, scoffing to hide the tremor in his tone. "I don't like the way this feels. It feels as if the whole world is holding its breath."

The words echoed faintly, *holding its breath.* The same phrase Balgair had used earlier. Perhaps they were right; perhaps even the gods were waiting, unseen.

"Amen to that, Lieu," Ben murmured from the back. "I've never seen it this dark, even outside at its darkest. This is unnatural."

There was a faint scratching sound. "Are you okay, Methak?" he asked, his voice low. "Talk to me, brother."

A cough. "Yeah, I'm fine." Methak's voice was steady but strained, as though pulled from the edge of a dream. "Can we get this done?"

Balgair shuddered. The air was thick, as though the darkness itself leaned on him.

Then Rique's irreverent voice broke through, bright as flint striking stone. "This reminds me of that crypt in Rouls."

Farank grunted, half laughing, half swearing. "Hush, thief. Ye're scaring Arien."

The enchantress shivered and clung closer to her bond. "I haven't thought of that little adventure in several years." She breathed the words like a confession. "That crypt was, chilling."

Balgair barely heard them. The scratching sound came again, and for an instant his mind conjured shapes in the dark, fingers dragging across stone, bones scraping through dust. He swallowed hard, reminding himself that imagination could be deadlier than any undead thing.

He pressed onward, hand on the wall, foot searching for the next step.

"How much further to the bottom?" Arien's voice trembled. "This darkness isn't natural, and it feels like it's trying to drown me. Does that make sense?"

"Yes," Balgair answered softly. "I was thinking it feels like the roof is trying to bury me." He dropped his tone to a whisper, as though afraid to wake something ancient. "To Ifrinn with this."

He pulled a rounded stone from his belt pouch and dropped it. The sound echoed faintly, plink, plink, plink, plink, and then silence devoured it.

Four steps. Four fading notes swallowed by a godless dark.

"Oy, what was that?" Farank called, his voice wary.

"Just a stone," Balgair replied. "I think we have four steps left. Then we'll be at the bottom." He hesitated, then prayed, [Please, my lady, let me be right.]

The silence that answered him was worse than mockery, it was indifference.

He took the next step down. Solid wood underfoot. His hand brushed the wall, cool and slick with damp. His heartbeat was a drum echoing inside his skull.

Third step. Another deep breath.

He prayed to every god he could name, not for victory, but for footing. [Please, please, please, let it be solid ground.]

His boot found earth, but his searching hand found no corner, only more wall, smooth and endless.

The darkness was complete, and the world felt weightless, unanchored.

He stood there for a long moment, breathing hard, the others breathing with him. The quiet between them was not silence anymore—it was presence. It pressed against their skin like water, waiting for one of them to move, to break the spell.

Balgair exhaled and muttered, "Still dark."

The sound vanished into the black. He had reached the bottom, but not the end.

And somewhere beyond that sightless space, something ancient was listening.

"Damn this darkness. Balgair, are you off the steps?" Brandyn's voice came low and tight, the old soldier's composure fraying at the edges. Fear lived in everyone's lungs now, breathing with them.

Balgair shook his head, then remembered no one could see him. "Yes, I'm off the step but can't see beyond my feet." He hesitated, truth rising unbidden. "To be fair, I can't even see my feet. So, when you get down here, be careful. We don't know what's around us."

He didn't add the rest: that he feared stepping on Heather's still body, that every silence was an accusation from the dark. He strained for a breath, for a heartbeat, anything that would prove she was still alive.

Something brushed his shoulder, and Brandyn's voice followed it. "We wouldn't want to step on the captain's bond." The words came as the tavern master took a halting step forward and cursed softly when his boot struck something unseen.

Another brush, another body moving past in the gloom,followed by muffled swearing as someone met the wall.

"This isn't going to work," Arien whispered. Her breath was warm against Balgair's ear as she leaned into him from behind. "We need light. It's just a shame that *Draoidheacd* is blocked." She sighed and started to move away.

"Hold on a minute," Balgair muttered, catching her wrist. A memory surfaced like a candle spark. He released her and rifled through his pouch. "Can it be chemical light?"

"Chemical?" Arien repeated, the word alien on her tongue. "What do you—?" She stopped, eyes widening as a soft click and shake broke the suffocating black. The vial bloomed with a faint, ghostly light. The first thing he saw was her face, pale, astonished, alive.

Balgair handed her the vial. The glow painted her fingers in silver. "Maighstir Darkblade mentioned something about bioluminescence," he said. "Like certain lichen that glow in caves."

Arien's expression softened into awe. "Yes," she breathed. "Yes, I think I can make this work." She cupped the vial in her right hand and lifted the other above it. Her voice trembled with invocation:

"Parva lux rutilans. Tardus et stabilis adolebitque et crescere splendesco quasi meridianus lux."

For a moment, the light shivered as if deciding whether to live. Then it swelled, steady and pure, and the room drew its first breath in hours.

Shapes emerged from shadow—crates, tables, vials. Faces flickered into being, pale as ghosts rediscovering themselves.

A voice broke the stunned silence: "About time." Then another, rough with disbelief. "Hey, Captain, I think I found Heather."

Balgair turned, the new light reflecting in his eyes like the memory of sunrise. Heather lay crumpled near the edge of an etched circle carved into the stone floor. He dismissed the runes with a glance and sprinted to her side.

Dropping to one knee, he checked her pulse with the care of a man afraid to feel nothing. Her skin was cold but alive. The touch restored something beyond heartbeat and breath—it restored *time*.

The moment his hand met hers, the silence cracked. Ananke's presence surged back like floodwater, her concern blooming in his mind, sharp, sweet, divine.

[I'm okay, Milady. Can you tell me what happened?]

Her reply was not words but emotion, sorrow and vigilance. He felt her reach outward, her awareness brushing against her kin. The world was stirring again.

"That's more like it," Methak muttered, relief in his tone. Ben nodded beside him, his voice quieter but reverent.

"Mixcoatl's awake again. Even down here under two hundred bodies of stone... it's like the air's moving."

"Touch nothing!" Arien barked suddenly. Her eyes roved the chamber, cataloguing the clutter. "There are vials everywhere, draoidheil components. If any spill, we could—"

"—blow ourselves up, aye," Farank finished, still pressed flat against the wall. "I'll stay right here, thank you kindly."

"Yeah, yeah, we gotcha," Methak said, skirting the crates with exaggerated care. "Just wondering where they kept the armory."

"It won't be in here," Arien replied without looking at him. "Only an idiot would keep steel near draoidheil glass."

"This building's full of thieves, assassins, whores, and undesirables," Brandyn reminded her dryly.

"That may be so," Arien countered, "but Brigid wasn't an idiot."

Their voices filled the chamber, the sound of *ordinary life* creeping back into the sacred hush.

Balgair barely heard them. He rolled Heather gently onto her back and searched her body for wounds. Finding none, he reached into his pouch, pulling out a square of cloth. His canteen was punctured, empty.

"Arien, is there any plain water in all this mess?" he called.

She stopped mid-argument and turned toward him. Seeing him cradling Heather, she softened. "There should be. Let me look."

Moments later, she returned with a bowl of water. "Here you go, sir."

"Thank you," he whispered, dipping the cloth and brushing it across Heather's forehead. "Come on, *Mo te Álainn,* wake up."

He lifted her gently into his lap. For a heartbeat, nothing. Then a sound, small, human, miraculous.

"Ungh..." Her eyes fluttered open. "I have such a headache." She blinked slowly, voice barely a breath. "You came for me."

Balgair smiled, caught between disbelief and devotion. When her hand rose to cup his cheek, the world narrowed to that touch—the warmth, the light, the weight of all that had nearly been lost.

"She said you'd move mountains to find me."

Her whisper trembled between them, fragile as dawn.

And for the first time since the darkness began, the world answered, a quiet hum beneath their feet, the breath of the gods returning to the mortal plane.

Balgair nodded, knowing exactly who she meant, even as he felt the faint, satisfied ripple of emotion from Ananke, a warmth like a smile carried on a divine current.

Her presence was alive again within him, humming softly, proud and unspoken.

"I'm sorry I didn't believe her," Heather said in a small, trembling voice. She searched his eyes, looking for the reason behind his madness, the why beneath the courage. "Why would you do it?"

"Because a certain blonde-haired and blue-eyed woman asked me to save her," Balgair replied, a trace of a grin curving his lips, "and I couldn't refuse her."

At that, Heather's cheeks flushed, and she buried her face against his chest as though to hide from both the light and his answer.

"You could have died," she whispered, her voice muffled against the coarse fabric of his tunic.

He nodded, the motion gentle but sure. "It would have been worth it." He drew her closer, arms wrapping around her in quiet certainty. "Neither Amelia nor Nell would ever forgive me if I let a woman die."

Heather's breath caught. She couldn't quite believe what she heard, that this rough, stubborn man had risked everything for her. Tears welled, slipping unbidden down her cheeks, tracing the dirt and exhaustion that clung to her face.

"There, there, *mo tè àlainn,*" Balgair murmured, the old Saorsan endearment falling from his lips like a benediction. "It's okay."

His voice was low, reassuring, as if the sound itself could weave a ward around her.

Heavy footsteps approached, the steady rhythm of a soldier returning to duty. A familiar voice broke the spell.

"What happened to Brigid and Yarsmith?" Brandyn asked, his tone steady but tinged with concern.

Heather lifted her head from Balgair's chest and found the tavern master standing over them, shadow framed in the soft, lingering light of Arien's spell.

Suddenly aware of herself, she stammered, "I don't know, *maighstir* Brandyn. I must have passed out, because the last thing I remember is the darkness reaching for me."

She clung to Balgair for a few more breaths, then drew in a steadying one. "Can we get out of here? I want to go back to the Inn."

"Of course we can," Balgair said as he rose, helping her gently to her feet. "What do you think, Lieutenant?"

"It would be a good idea if we got out of here before we have to fight our way out," Brandyn replied, already scanning the shadows.

Balgair gave a quiet nod and turned to where the ranger was standing near the stairway. "Care to lead the way?"

The ranger nodded once and started up the stairs, his boots thudding softly against wood and stone.

Methak waited until he was halfway up before following. "This is certainly easier than it was in the dark," he said with a grin, his tone light for the first time in what felt like hours.

Heather blinked and turned toward Balgair, eyes wide with disbelief. "You came down those stairs in the dark?"

When he nodded, her astonishment sharpened into exasperation. "Are you insane? You all could have fallen!"

"Yeah, well," Arien said with a wink, stepping closer, "there was this beautiful woman to save. So the men thought it was worth the risk."

Heather's blush deepened, her hand instinctively finding Balgair's. She grasped it tightly, a fragile thread of warmth between them. "You're insane, you know that, right?"

Balgair gave her hand a reassuring squeeze, his grin soft and genuine.

Heather's heart lifted, a song of relief and gratitude rising in her chest where fear had once lived. She watched as Arien and Farank began their ascent, their quiet laughter echoing faintly against the stone.

Brandyn followed next, steady and deliberate. Balgair was just behind him, one hand still holding Heather's. She hesitated only once, at the threshold.

For an instant, her eyes flicked back over her shoulder.

The magic circle still shimmered faintly in the dim light, a cold echo of what had nearly claimed her. She shuddered, drawing in a sharp breath, thankful beyond words that it had not been her tomb.

Then she turned away and began to climb, following the sound of her companions, the warmth of their laughter, and the faint, living pulse of light above.

Behind her, the basement fell silent once more. The circle's faint glow dimmed, as though the darkness itself bowed its head in defeat.

And somewhere far beyond sight, Ananke's presence whispered through the stillness, a quiet, pleased hum, like the tightening of a single link in a divine chain.

Chapter Ten

The Quiet Between Storms

It was far easier to get Heather out of the building than it had been to get to her. The path upward felt almost unreal, as though the shadows themselves, now sated, allowed them to pass. The air carried a chill that spoke of endings, and of the quiet that follows the turning of a great wheel.

All they had to do was exit the basement and walk down the hall to the outside door, where five members of the town guard waited, their cloaks dripping in the soft, persistent snow.

When Balgair stepped into the open air, he felt the weight of the world return.

The darkness had clung to him like breathless fear; now, the cool sting of snow was its absolution. Each flake was a whisper of the gods, cleansing but not commanding, the subtle mark of *Saorsa's silence*, that sacred freedom when the divine steps back and lets mortals walk their own road.

Brandyn stood near one of the guards, gesturing toward him. A single raindrop struck Balgair's forehead, cold and deliberate, and he glanced skyward as if to seek some hidden meaning. When none came, he wiped the rain from his face and approached the guardsman.

"Yes? How may I help you?"

"Did you get what you went in there for?" the guardsman asked, his gaze flicking toward Heather.

She blushed and lowered her head, as though the weight of attention were too heavy after so much darkness.

"I did," Balgair confirmed, his voice steady, protective. He placed an arm around her shoulders, a simple human act, but in the eyes of *Saorsa*, every touch of care was a covenant. The gods had withdrawn, yes, but love had not.

The guardsman saluted, his discipline like an echo of the order the world once knew before the gods fell silent. He relaxed when Balgair returned the gesture. "Sir, we are sorry it took us so long to get here. We had to pull men from their posts when the call sounded." His tone held remorse, and something more, that quiet mortal yearning to serve something greater.

"Sir, have you heard what happened to our Sheriff and his deputies?"

Balgair thought back to what Huitzilopochtli had told him. "Yes. Lord Huitzilopochtli said he'd been killed in a fight."

The guardsman's shoulders loosened, as though the simple confirmation of tragedy allowed him to breathe again. "Yes, sir." His eyes lingered on Balgair, reading the scars and insignia as though they were holy runes.

A faint smile tugged at his lips when he saw the four chevrons on the mercenary's shield. "Sir, normally I wouldn't ask this, but have you considered taking the job? We could really use your help, sir."

The snow thickened, and for a heartbeat the world hushed, a moment suspended between divine watchfulness and human choice. In Saorsa's creed, it is in such pauses that destiny holds its breath. The guardsman's request was no mere plea; it was the voice of the world itself, asking Balgair to stand in the gods' stead.

Heather held her breath as Balgair's arm tightened around her for a moment, then eased. She dared to look up, hope flickering in her eyes like a fragile lamp. She knew he would go wherever his path demanded, and that her own was now tied to his, whether by fate or by faith.

"What do you think, mo tè àlainn?" he asked quietly, his tone gentler than the rain. The divine name passed between them like a blessing, unseen and warm.

391

"I wouldn't dare to speak for you, sir." Her soft voice trembled, though not from fear. To the eyes of Saorsa, this was the first stirrings of agency, the humility before the awakening of one's own will.

Balgair grunted. "Some help you are, woman," he teased, the rough edges of his voice softening the moment. It was in such small exchanges, the laughter in the rain, the teasing of the weary, that mortal love became its own act of worship.

Heather coughed and leaned into him. The warmth of his body, the steadiness of his breath, reminded her that she still belonged to the living world. She felt the rain in her hair, running down her neck, and for the first time since her capture, she shivered not from fear, but from the fragile return of feeling.

Not getting a response from her, Balgair sighed softly. "I'll be here for a day or two," he said at last, glancing at the guardsman's shoulder. "Sergeant. I'll make up my mind before then and let you know, or let someone know."

The guardsman nodded, a hint of relief softening his formality. "That's about what I figured, sir. I'd be lying if I said that we didn't need someone who understood how we think." He hesitated, almost embarrassed by his own honesty. "The Sheriff was a good man, but he didn't understand the military, sir."

Balgair nodded again, the rain tracing down his jaw like liquid resolve. "Thank you, sergeant." He felt Heather's shivering worsen. "If you don't mind, we'll be going before the young lady gets too cold."

"Of course, sir." The guardsman saluted again, as though sending a prayer through gesture. He watched as the small group departed, vanishing into the rain-dimmed street, mortals carrying the quiet of gods upon their shoulders.

By the time they reached the inn, the rain had soaked through every stitch of clothing and left Heather trembling. The storm clung to her like memory, cold, heavy, inescapable. She tried to keep her cough contained, but when it broke loose, she nearly doubled over, each convulsion shaking more than her lungs.

Arien wasn't much better off, though the weight of her *maighstir's* cloak kept the worst of the chill at bay.

Balgair caught Heather before she fell. Without hesitation, without thought, even, he swept her into his arms.

The gesture felt as natural as breathing. In *Saorsa's* light, such acts were not merely kindness; they were sacred impulses, love made manifest in motion.

Mortified, Heather wanted to tell him to put her down, but her body betrayed her, weak and unsteady. She let her head rest against his chest, the sound of his heartbeat steady beneath her ear, the mortal drum of safety. "I'm sorry, Maighstir. I don't want to be a burden."

He carried her into the inn's common room, the scent of firewood and warm bread wrapping around them like absolution. "It's okay, *mo tè àlainn.*" His voice gentled the air, and for the first time since the cellar, the tension in her shoulders loosened.

Across the room, laughter sparked. Lucy ran forward, skirts whispering, and flung herself into Brandyn's waiting arms. "I'm so glad you made it back," she breathed, voice trembling with relief.

The barkeep laughed softly, the sound of a man rediscovering joy. "I told you we'd be back." He held her close, marveling at how perfectly her small frame fit against his, as though every piece of the world was finding its rightful place again.

Balgair set his shield down on a table, the metallic clink echoing through the room. He began unfastening his chain shirt, the links heavy with water and exhaustion. "I hate to ask, Lieutenant, but can we borrow more clothes for Heather?" He gestured toward the shivering woman.

Lucy turned immediately, kindness lighting her face. "Of course, Maighstir Balgair. I'll grab her a change of clothes and take her upstairs."

He nodded to her, then turned back to Heather and drew her gently close. "I want you to go with Lucy. Get cleaned up and then get some sleep." When she opened her mouth to protest, he stopped her with a look, firm, but not unkind. "You need it."

She knew that look. If she refused, he would simply carry her upstairs, bathe her himself, and tuck her into bed like a stubborn child. Knowing this, and knowing that his tenderness would undo her completely, she acquiesced and followed Lucy up the stairs, her footsteps soft and uncertain.

After sending Arien off to get cleaned up, Farank ambled toward the bar, shaking the rain from his hair. "How about some ale?"

The barkeep, still half-lost in Lucy's laughter, filled his order absently. Farank's axe and shield went back to their accustomed place on the wall, a small, comforting symbol that the world was once again as it should be.

Ben ordered two drinks and carried them to Balgair's table. "Mind if we join you?"

Seeing the ranger and the archer with weary grins and twin mugs, Balgair nodded. "Be my guests."

"I think you could use this," Ben said, sliding a drink toward him. His tone was easy, but the look in his eyes carried the unspoken weight of brotherhood forged in blood. "And I'll have you know that if you don't ask Heather to bond with you, we'll take you outside and attempt to beat you up."

Balgair lifted the mug, studying him over the rim. "You'll attempt to beat me up?" His grin was dry, a spark of mischief breaking through his fatigue. "I've seen the two of you fight. If you wanted to beat me, I probably wouldn't get close enough to hit you."

The ranger chuckled and took a sip. "Do you intend to ask her to bond with you?"

Balgair drank slowly, the ale rich and grounding after so much cold. He swallowed and nodded. "I do. Otherwise, I wouldn't have gone after her."

"Good," Methak said, leaning back in his chair. "That's the important question out of the way. That just leaves one other thing."

Balgair already knew what it was. He'd been turning it over in his mind since Huitzilopochtli mentioned it, since the guardsman had echoed it outside in the rain. "The Sheriff's job, right?"

Ben nodded, about to speak when Brandyn, Farank, and Riq joined them.

"Have you brought it up yet?" Brandyn asked.

"We were just going to discuss it," Ben replied.

Brandyn nodded, stretching his legs beneath the table. The inn's light pooled over their faces, a mortal constellation of tired eyes and steady resolve. Ben leaned forward. "Before you apply for the position, you should know the whole story."

"You've got my attention," Balgair said, glancing around the table. "Let me hear it."

"I don't want to speak ill of the dead," Ben began, his tone reverent. "Dafyd was a good man. He knew the law and his people, but he didn't understand the guard or the military, and it showed."

Methak nodded, sipping his ale in quiet agreement. The air thickened with memory.

"For the first five years of his contract, things were good," Ben continued. "Then the thieves and assassins hit town and formed their guilds."

Balgair suspected where this was going, but said nothing.

"At first, Dafyd tried to chase them out," Ben went on. "When that failed, he made two deals. The first was that if they didn't kill anyone while stealing, they wouldn't be hunted down and killed. He'd arrest them and hold them until bail."

Balgair nodded. "That sounds reasonable. What was the second?"

Methak glanced at Ben before taking up the tale. "He let them run the whorehouses, as long as taxes were paid."

"Interesting," Balgair said, his expression unreadable. "What went wrong?"

"Brutus took over the thieves' guild," Brandyn explained grimly, "and let chaos reign. When Dafyd warned him, Brutus sct a trap that killed him and his four deputies. After that, he thought himself untouchable."

Balgair's face was carved from stillness as he listened. "Out of curiosity, how did Heather fit into all of this?"

Silence descended. It wasn't the silence of guilt, but of pain too deep to tread upon lightly.

"Well, that isn't good," Balgair murmured. "Care to share?"

No one moved.

"I've never seen a group of men that didn't want to talk about something." He turned to Brandyn. "Spill it, Lieutenant."

Brandyn sighed heavily. "Brutus wanted Heather for his whorehouse. When she refused, he killed her family and wouldn't leave her alone."

Balgair's eyes darkened. "Ahh." His tone carried the weight of understanding, and sorrow. "She tried to run, but got caught and raped, didn't she?"

Brandyn nodded.

Balgair exhaled through his nose, long and quiet. "If I take the job, how much support will I get?"

"As much as you need from us," Methak answered at once. "The guardsmen will back you, the Sheriff's department too. Though you might have trouble with the mayor and the town *magaidh*. Both fled before Dafyd was killed. Haven't been back since."

Balgair shook his head. "Surely there are others better qualified for the post. Why me?"

Riq leaned forward, his voice steady. "You went in after Heather and got her out without killing too many people." A faint smile ghosted across his lips. "More importantly, you got out alive."

"By blind damned luck," Balgair muttered. Then, softer, "However, if you're sure about it, I'll check into it tomorrow." He pushed his mug away and stood, his shadow long in the lamplight.

"I'm going to get some sleep. I'll see you gents in the morning."

After cleaning up, Heather lingered by the window, listening to the soft murmur of rain against the glass. The world outside was gray and calm, washed clean after a night of terror and storm. When Balgair didn't come up, she lay down for a moment, intending only to rest her eyes. But exhaustion claimed her gently, like a warm tide.

When she awoke, she found herself tucked beneath a comforter, wrapped in a cocoon of warmth. The air in the room carried the faint scent of leather, steel, and smoke, the scent of him. For a long time, she lay still, her heartbeat slow and steady, before sitting up and stretching.

The ache in her body was dulled now, replaced by something softer, the peace that comes after surviving.

A low snore drew her attention. She followed the sound and found Balgair asleep on the couch, his cloak draped over him like a shadowed wing. For a moment she only stood and watched.

The lines of battle and burden had eased from his face; in sleep, he looked almost boyish, untouched by the world's cruelty. A strange tenderness rose within her chest, not desire, not yet, but something deeper, older: a quiet recognition of safety.

When he mumbled something in his dream, warmth coursed through her like sunlight through glass.

She smiled faintly. Smoothing the wrinkles from the simple dress Lucy had lent her, she gave him one last look before slipping quietly downstairs.

In the kitchen, she moved without thought, her hands guided by memory and care. She did not know what he liked, only that she wanted to make something that would please him. Bread, fruit, porridge, a bit of cheese, small things, humble things. The work steadied her. By the time she returned upstairs, her arms bore a tray filled with warmth and fragrance.

She opened the door softly. The morning light was gentler now, filtering through the curtains and resting across Balgair's face. She smiled, without reason, without thinking, and placed the tray on the small table beside the couch.

It just felt right to kneel and wait for him to wake, to offer this quiet devotion freely.

As the sunbeam traced his features, she fought the sudden urge to reach out and touch him. Her fingers trembled, but she held still. Reverence, not need, guided her now.

The first thing Balgair saw upon waking was Heather kneeling at the foot of the couch, watching him. The second thing he noticed was the smile on her face, then the slight blush as she caught him watching her. "Good Morrow, Maighstir," she whispered. "How did you sleep?"

Balgair pushed himself upright, his hair tousled, his expression soft with sleep. "Not bad. How do you feel this morning?"

He studied her face, the pallor of exhaustion gone, the brightness of life returned.

"I feel well, Maighstir," she said, still smiling. "Are you hungry?" Her question carried more than concern; it was a plea for purpose, for proof that she could still do something good.

He was about to deny his hunger, but his stomach spoke first, rumbling loud enough to make her giggle. He surrendered with a crooked grin. "I'm famished."

She gazed at him, eyes bright. "I didn't know what you liked to eat, so I made you a little of everything," she admitted, rising to her feet and retrieving the tray. "I hope you'll find something you like."

Balgair looked over the offering, the careful arrangement of simple food. "It looks good," he said, picking up a bowl of hot cereal and fruit. "I'm betting you haven't eaten yet." Her blush confirmed it. "I'm not going to be able to eat all of this. Why don't you have some?"

Her blue eyes flicked to him, uncertain but hopeful. "Thank you, maighstir," she mumbled, taking a piece of bread and wrapping it around a slice of meat.

They ate together in silence. It was a tender, sacred kind of quiet , the kind that exists between souls who no longer need to speak to be understood. The morning light turned golden as it touched the edge of the tray, gilding their shared meal.

It was, in its own way, communion ,
not between mortal and god, but between
two wounded beings learning how to be
whole.

When the food was gone, Balgair
leaned back, content. "You did a great
job," he said, handing her his empty plate
and watching her set it aside.

"Thank you, maighstir. My mother
was always afraid that I wouldn't be able to
cook to a man's satisfaction." Her voice
trembled as the past crept in. The smile
faltered; the old wound reopened.

Before she knew it, she was in his lap,
tears spilling freely. "I miss them,
Maighstir. I was so mean to them."

Balgair froze for only a heartbeat
before his instincts, no, his compassion,
took over.

He held her close, whispering softly, the way a man speaks to calm a frightened child or a restless spirit.

When her sobs quieted, she wiped her cheeks and sat back, embarrassed. "You must think I'm a mess."

He shook his head slowly. "I don't think that at all. I think you are a woman who hasn't had time to mourn her parents yet." He brushed her tears away with the back of his hand. "It's okay to cry, *mo tè àlainn.*"

Heather leaned into his touch, drawn by the gentleness in his voice. "Why are you so nice to me?"

He tilted his head slightly. "How did you expect me to act?"

Her breath hitched as the memory of Brutus surfaced. "I don't know. The last man I trusted killed my parents and raped me."

The words hung between them like smoke. Balgair's eyes darkened; his breath grew tight. Anger burned through him, sharp and red, but it was not for her. "Not all men are like Brutus," he said, fighting to keep his voice calm. His jaw tightened as he closed his eyes, forcing the rage back into its cage.

Heather lowered her gaze. "I know," she whispered. "I'm sorry I made you mad."

"I'm not angry, *mo tè àlainn*," he murmured, steady again. "You could never make me mad."

Her lips trembled as she tried to smile. "I always find a way to make someone mad at me. Why should you be any different?"

He looked at her for a long moment. "Because I—" He hesitated, the truth forming carefully. "My goddess, she's so much a part of my life that I can't hurt someone who doesn't deserve it." A quiet smile softened his face. "If Amelia and Nell were here, you could talk to them and find out why I'm different."

Heather drew a slow breath, studying him. He looked impossibly human, worn and imperfect, and yet somehow radiant. His hair was tousled, his brown eyes deep with warmth. [He can't be that perfect.]

She hadn't reached for Ananke since before the darkness. Yet now, the goddess's mezzo-soprano voice slid through her mind like silk. [Why are you denying what you feel?]

Heather closed her eyes. [I've been hurt too many times to believe in perfect.]

Ananke's tone carried quiet amusement. [He's not perfect. He's *real*. That's the point. He cares for you.]

[But why does he care? I'm nobody.]

The goddess's voice chilled, a whisper of winter wind. [We aren't discussing this again.]

Heather buried her face in her hands, not noticing that Balgair was watching her with quiet concern. [Why me? What's so special about me?]

[You are balance, *mo neach briste.* You bridge what he cannot. He and his bhanna need you.]

[Balance?] Heather almost laughed aloud. [What can I bring to them that they don't already have?]

She could feel Ananke's smugness, like a smile in the dark. [Trust me, little one. You'll like them.]

Heather sighed softly, the sound barely audible. She lifted her eyes to the morning light, feeling its warmth on her skin.

[As you wish, Milady,] she surrendered.

The light seemed to glow brighter in response, not divine, but simple and human, the light of a day beginning anew.

And for the first time in a long while, Heather didn't feel like a burden.

She felt seen.

She felt free.

Chapter Eleven

Seeds of Shadow, Bonds of Light

he cave breathed dust and memory. Shadows clung to the rough stone like forgotten prayers, and the air smelled faintly of iron, old blood and time's slow decay. Brigid stood at the center of it, her heart fluttering with both awe and unease as she watched the ancient being shape the unseen. Reality bent where his gestures passed, ripples in the stillness of the world.

She had expected revelation, light, perhaps, or divine music, but there was only dust and the rasp of eternity. She was ecstatic that they had freed him, that he had named her his High Priestess, yet some part of her felt cheated. Divinity, it turned out, was neither beautiful nor kind.

The black-robed form barely moved as it turned toward her. Beneath the deep cowl, two red eyes glowed like embers of a dying fire. "Is something amiss?" The voice that came from the darkness was parched and hollow, as though it had not tasted water, or mercy, for a thousand years.

Brigid hesitated, her mouth drawing into a line that trembled on the edge of a pout. "Not really, Maighstir. I'm just mourning the loss of my life's work." The words escaped her lips before she could call them back. Even as she spoke them, she remembered who she addressed, a being whose very name could wither mortals to dust.

The god's eyes flickered, blinked, perhaps, and the cave seemed to draw tighter around them. "What loss? We will be going back soon."

The witch blinked, startled. "We will?" Her voice carried fragile hope, the kind that shatters easily.

"Of course." The cowl dipped in slow affirmation. "As soon as I talk to my other follower, we'll go back. The people in that building will be among my first followers. Between the inhabitants and the two guilds represented, there should be enough people to cement my patronage."

The words curled through the air like incense, heady, suffocating. Brigid found herself leaning closer, her pulse quickening as if under enchantment.

"Oh, good. I had to leave all of my wands, staves, tinctures, potions, and poisons behind when we ran. I was not looking forward to having to replace them."

The cowl dipped again, the faintest hint of amusement in the motion. "From what I could tell some of them were quite rare and irreplaceable." He reached out, and his gloved fingers, impossibly cold, brushed against her chin. "We will go back in time." His tone darkened, became heavy with venom. "No mercenary is going to chase me out."

A shiver ran through Brigid. The vindictive promise in his voice sank into her bones like frost. This was no benevolent Diathan of freedom and fate, this was something older, boundless, and starved.

"How many followers do you need to reclaim your place with the other Diathan?" she asked softly. Even now, curiosity conquered caution. She had worshiped gods all her life, but never spoken to one face-to-face. She would not waste the chance.

The ancient god's red eyes flared. He studied her openly, the curve of her form, the shimmer of her hair, the pulse beneath her throat. He measured her as one might measure an offering.

She was beautiful, yes, but beauty to him was currency, not grace. He had seen such women before, the ambitious, the yearning, those who would trade flesh for power and call it devotion.

"A hundred or so is a good starting point," he said at last, his tone as casual as a merchant tallying profit. "

After that, each soul is a way to increase my personal power. The more worshippers a god has, the more he can do, the more favors he can dispense."As he spoke, his fingers moved idly, flickering like a weaver counting threads. But these were not threads of destiny. They were strands of a web.

Brigid leaned forward, rapt. "If it doesn't offend you too much, how did you get imprisoned? Who locked you away?"

The god stilled. His hands clenched into fists, and the air around him seemed to contract. When he spoke, his words carried the weight of millennia. "My brother tricked me and imprisoned me in Skull Cap/ If he weren't already dead, I'd hunt him down and wrap him in my webs."

The words were cold and terrible, not sorrow but hatred that had fermented into madness. The shadows stirred, whispering as if afraid. Before his rage could bloom fully, the god exhaled and forced himself calm. "Even though I have no quarrel with these Diathan, I have no desire to face them until I regain my power."

He stepped toward Brigid, slow and deliberate, like a tide advancing on the shore. When he slipped an arm around her, she felt the chill of eternity against her skin. "If you don't want to spend the night in my bed, you had better say so, my High Priestess."

Brigid's breath caught. His words were both command and invitation, the seduction of power dressed as choice.

Her body flushed with the warmth of awe and terror, and she pressed herself against him without thinking. "Yes, maighstir," she crooned, her voice trembling with devotion and need. "Always, yes."

The cave dimmed as they moved toward the bedroll, and the shadows seemed to draw closer, as if eager to witness the unholy sacrament. In that act, worship and submission became indistinguishable, not love, but consumption disguised as reverence.

From the far wall, two men watched in silence. The assassin leaned against the stone, arms crossed, his eyes cold and unreadable. The tall man beside him shifted the weight of his bec de' corbin before setting it down.

"That didn't take her long, did it?" he muttered, his tone as casual as if commenting on the weather.

Yarsmith sank lower, resting his head against his chest. "Nope, it didn't, Tom. Do me a favor and wake me when it's time to move on."

Tom nodded, his expression half grim, half amused, and watched as the god and the witch entangled themselves in the flickering light.

"What are we going to do if he plants a child in her belly?" he asked after a while, conversationally, as though the thought of a demigod offspring was a practical inconvenience.

Yarsmith shrugged. "The same thing we'd do if it was yours or mine , not a damn thing."

He tried to ignore the low moans that echoed through the cavern. "She's an adult and can handle her own problems."

Tom picked up his weapon and began to file the spike on the hammer's edge. The rasp of metal against stone filled the air. "I wonder what it would be like to have a god-child running around."

"I dunno," Yarsmith replied, his voice weary. "It isn't the first, and probably won't be the last." He pulled his cloak tighter around himself and closed his eyes.

The cave fell into uneasy quiet, punctuated only by the god's whispers and the slow scraping of steel. And in that silence, something ancient began to stir, not life, but hunger reborn.

The morning light had softened the edges of the world, gilding the room in quiet warmth. It fell over Heather like a benediction as she sat across from Balgair, her face streaked with the remnants of tears. What had begun as hysteria had softened to confusion, and now , slowly , to surrender. Not surrender to him, but to something higher, older, and far kinder.

Balgair could have stopped it. He had done so before, when mortals broke beneath the touch of the divine. But this was different. He felt Ananke's presence all around them, patient and watchful, her unseen hands guiding the moment toward something healing. The mercenary bowed his head slightly, as though before an altar, and allowed it to unfold.

Heather's chest rose and fell with a heavy sigh. "I can't win, can I?" she huffed, shaking her head. Her expression softened, and she tilted her head as though listening to something distant. "That's what I thought." A flicker of humor tugged at the corner of her mouth as she scooted away from him and met his gaze. "She tells me that I would be a fool to turn you away."

Balgair nearly laughed , a sharp, reflexive thing that he swallowed before it could escape. "Milady is a good judge of character, but she won't kick you out for not agreeing with her."

Heather's laughter bubbled up like water over stone. "She won't kick me out," she said between breaths. "Either you have a strange sense of humor, or she does, because she told me that what she could do would make my life, so far, seem like a picnic."

The mercenary blinked. That did not sound like the goddess he knew. [Did you really say that, Milady?]

A familiar warmth unfurled behind his eyes , laughter like silver bells in a cathedral.

[Yes, I did, my Balgair,] came the amused reply. He could almost see her smiling at him. [I have plans for you and her.] A pause, filled with the scent of rosemary and the faintest rustle of silk. [The exact details are still to be hammered out.]

Then the fragrance deepened , wild herbs, mountain air , and he felt the ghost of arms around his shoulders. [Why don't I leave the two of you alone so that you can figure out what you both want?]

And just like that, she was gone. The warmth faded, leaving the soft quiet of a mortal room behind.

Heather's breath caught under his stare. Her hands fluttered nervously down her dress, smoothing fabric that was already flawless. "Do we even have a choice at all?" she asked, voice low, head bowed.

Balgair's heart clenched. He wanted to tell her yes , that she had always had a choice , but he sensed that what she needed wasn't reassurance, but truth.

"Nan Diathan always say that we have a choice in how we live our lives," he said slowly. Her blue eyes lifted, doubtful and searching. "In reality, I've come to realize that we can make whatever choices we desire, but in the end, we always inadvertently do just what they said we would do."

Heather laughed, but the sound was brittle, tinged with pain. "She wants me to give you my bond." Her back straightened, her defiance tempered by fear. Crawling off his lap, she sank to her knees, the posture both humble and human. "Doesn't she understand how hard that will be?"

He could see the ache in her eyes, the weight of too many lost certainties. "Nan Diathan were around before the world was," he said, "and I think they've forgotten how we think." His tone softened, almost apologetic. "They try to think like we do, but it's like us trying to communicate with an animal."

At once, a flicker of amused chastisement brushed his mind , the mental equivalent of being thumped on the back of the head.

Heather's bitter laugh came again. "So, are we the animals, and don't truly understand them?"

He winced, rubbing the back of his neck. "No. Maybe like one of us talking to a child would be more apt."

Her eyes narrowed with disbelief. "What if I don't want to bond with any man?" Her voice trembled, more out of memory than conviction.

"That's your choice," Balgair said gently. "How can I convince you that I won't force you to do something against your will?" He realized the misstep the instant the words left his mouth, but there was no taking them back.

A strange light flickered behind her eyes , not divine, but deeply human. She leaned forward, cautious and curious. "Tell me about your Bhanna."

Balgair groaned softly. "Well crap," he muttered under his breath. The gods might laugh at fate, but mortals had to live with it. "What do you want to know?"

"I want to know how you met them," she said, voice steady now. "Please, I need to know the real you."

Her request hung in the air like a prayer. The mercenary's gaze drifted inward, his memories rising like smoke from a hearth long unlit. He heard himself ask, "Where should I start?"

Heather's eyes softened. She knew she was asking something painful, but she needed to understand the man her goddess had chosen for her. "Tell me about Amelia."

Balgair nodded slowly, his expression easing into reminiscence. "Amelia is Ciad-Ghin. She's about my age." His lips curved faintly in affection. "Amelia is about this tall," he said, lifting his hand to his shoulder, "with long, beautiful, fiery red hair and crystal green eyes."

"How did you meet?" she asked quietly.

The question hung in the sunlit stillness, a bridge between past and future , between two souls bound not by force, but by the gentle hand of fate.

Seven Years Earlier

The early spring moon rode high above the sleeping woods, its pale light dancing across a clearing veiled in mist and blood. The six black swans, Balgair and his chosen, moved among the fallen like silent shadows, their blades whispering through the dark. Where they passed, the night grew still again.

The caravan of slavers had thought themselves safe beneath the shroud of darkness, their wares bound and broken, destined for the shadow markets. Yet justice does not sleep. When word reached Balgair's ear, he gathered five of his finest, men who had walked the edge of honor beside him, and set their course to intercept.

His plan had been patient, a strike before dawn, swift and unseen. But patience perished with the sound of a woman's scream. In that moment, six eyes met, and one unspoken truth bound them: there are cries no just man can ignore.

They fell upon the camp like the night's own wrath. In heartbeats, a half-score slavers lay dead, their blades unblooded, their cruelty unavenged. The rest scattered or perished beneath the moon's silent witness. When at last the clamor faded, Balgair moved among the broken cages and found her, the source of the cry.

She lay bound to the earth, stripped of dignity, surrounded by men whose lust had met steel's retribution. He knelt beside her, the moonlight turning his face to marble.

"How is she?" he asked quietly.

"She's unconscious," his soldier replied, nudging one of the corpses away with his boot. "I don't think this was the first time she was raped." He pointed to the fading whip marks along her stomach.

Balgair said nothing. The silence between heartbeats was a prayer. With a blade gentler than a sigh, he cut the rawhide cords and gathered her into his arms. "It'll be okay," he murmured, brushing her hair behind her ear as he draped his cloak across her nakedness.

He remained with her as his men carried the dead into the forest to bury them without name or stone. Mercy demanded no monument.

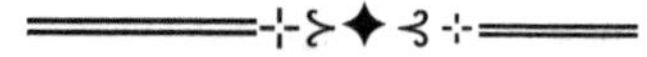

Time passed like breath in a story retold. Balgair's voice softened as he returned from memory. "At first, Amelia didn't want to have anything to do with any man, much less me. She would sit near me, but didn't want anything to do with me."

He smiled faintly, the ghost of the past warm upon him. "The first time I saw her smile was the night she returned my cloak to me. She said she wanted to meet the man who had saved them from a life of slavery. One thing led to another, and..." He looked upward, as though seeing the stars of that night again. "I think it was a year later when she offered her bond."

Heather's lips curved into a teasing smile. "You think it was a year later? You can't remember the day when you accepted her bond? That poor woman."

Balgair chuckled. "You're right. It was exactly a year, and I remember everything about that day." He turned his gaze on her. "Just as I'll remember everything about the day when you offer your bond."

"You seem very sure that I'm going to offer my bond to you," she teased again, though her heart fluttered beneath the jest.

"I have no doubt that you'll offer me your bond, and soon." His smile was playful, but his eyes were tender.

Heather fought back a blush, steadying her breath before asking, "What about Nell? What's the story?"

Balgair's expression darkened slightly, as though the memory bore a scar of its own. "That's easy. She was bonded to a mean bastard who used her to trick other men into one-on-one combats, so that he could kill them and take their property."

Heather caught the tremor beneath his calm. "There's got to be more to the story. Go on, please."

"It was actually Amelia who met her first. She came home, telling me about this poor woman that needed my help." His voice grew quiet. "When Amelia introduced her to me, I found myself wondering why this beautiful ebon-haired woman needed my help." His hands clenched at the memory.

"When I questioned her and she stripped away her clothes to show me the scars on her back and legs, I was ready to challenge her bond-master right there. But when she told us how he used his bond to mentally torture her,Milady was ready to kill him herself."

At that, the scent of rosemary filled the air, faint, ethereal, the invisible mark of Ananke's sympathy.

Balgair's tone softened. "After freeing her from her abusive master, I offered her sanctuary in my house." His smile returned, wistful. "It didn't take her long to bond with Amelia, and within six months, she offered her bond to me as well. We've been a happy family since then."

Heather's eyes shone with quiet envy and longing. *Love like that,* she thought, *might heal anything.*

"Do you think they'll accept me if I offer my bond?" she asked, her voice barely above a whisper, the tremor of hope betraying her attempt at calm.

Balgair could feel Ananke's soft humming in his mind, the goddess's anticipation shimmering like candlelight. He nodded, careful to keep his tone light. "I don't think they'll turn you down." His restraint was its own act of devotion. "What do you want, mo te alainn?"

Her gaze lingered on him, vulnerable and luminous. "I want someone who loves me enough to save me from myself."

The mercenary's eyes gentled. He gestured to the space near his left foot. "Go on."

"I want a strong man who I can look up to," she whispered, moving unconsciously toward the spot he indicated. "I want to surrender completely to him and make him happy." Her voice trembled, rich with feeling. "I want to bear his children."

She stopped, suddenly aware of how near she had come, and looked up into his face. "Is that man you?"

"That's for you to decide," Balgair said softly, the goddess's contented hum a chord beneath his words.

When he opened his arms, Heather came to him without thought. She curled into his lap, her head resting against his shoulder. The warmth between them was quiet, not consuming, the kind of warmth that builds a home.

"I so badly want you to be that man," she murmured, and he smiled against her hair.

When her breathing steadied, she lifted her head and pressed a soft kiss to his cheek. "I would love to give you my bond, but I can't... not yet."

Balgair stilled, waiting. Even Ananke paused, the air itself listening.

"If your Bhanna accept me," Heather said finally, "I will offer you my bond." Her eyes closed tightly, as though expecting refusal.

Instead, the mercenary felt the goddess's delighted sigh ripple through the unseen. [You just couldn't wait, could you?]

He could feel her laughter, fragrant and smug, as she reached out to his Bhanna across the ether. Then her attention turned toward Heather.

Whatever words Ananke spoke to her, Balgair did not hear. But he saw the blush bloom on Heather's cheeks, and he felt the warmth of her as she hid her face in his shoulder.

The air within the cave was still and cold, as though the night itself held its breath. A thin thread of moonlight slipped through a crack in the stone, spilling across the bedroll where divinity had defiled its promise.

Brigid rose in silence. The scent of dust and old power clung to her skin like the ghost of incense long since burned away. She adjusted her robes with trembling hands, each movement careful, almost reverent, as though she feared to wake what slept behind her.

The ancient god lay motionless, a shadow wrapped in darker cloth, but she could feel him even in stillness. His essence coiled inside her, burning and restless, like roots seeking to drink her marrow.

She turned away. She could not bear to meet the sight of him again.

When she crossed the cavern, Yarsmith and the tall man stirred from their half-sleep. The assassin's eyes were dull with exhaustion, yet he still found words.

"Not what you thought it would be?" he asked, his voice roughened by sand and cynicism.

The witch sank down beside them, her body heavy, her heart heavier still. "I can feel his seed taking root," she whispered, pressing a hand to her abdomen. Her face twisted in pain she tried to mask. "His potency will make me catch a child for sure."

The other man gazed at her, his expression unreadable in the gloom. Then he shrugged. "You made the choice, Brigid. You'll have to suffer the consequences." There was no cruelty in his tone — only weariness, the resignation of one who had seen too much of gods and their aftermath. "We'll help you the best we can, you know that."

Brigid grimaced, heat blooming in her belly. "I wanted power, not to be used." Her voice cracked as she spoke. "It's like I'm being scoured inside."

Yarsmith sighed softly, rolling to face the cave wall. "Get some sleep. I have a feeling that we'll be busy tomorrow."

The cavern fell quiet again, save for the soft breath of mortals adrift in uneasy dreams.

Brigid lay back and stared into the dark above her, but where others saw black stone, she saw nothingness. No whisper. No warmth. No rosemary-scented grace.

She reached out in her mind for the goddess who had once spoken to her through the veil, but there was only silence. The silence of judgment. The silence of a world that turns its face away.

Her thoughts circled the hollow ache inside her. *Would she be the mother of a demi-god, or would she have to forego the power she'd spent a lifetime chasing?*

She did not know. The heat within her was neither life nor death, but something older, a mingling of creation and corruption.

In her mind, she saw a web of shadowed threads, and at its center, something stirring. Not divine. Not human. Merely inevitable.

Brigid closed her eyes, her last thought dissolving into the dark: perhaps the true punishment for ambition was not destruction, but to carry its consequence within you,and call it *hope*.

Chapter Twelve

The Keys of Greim Claigeann

It was rare that the gods met face to face, but the recent events had brought them together in Astinmah's forest home. Her dwelling was no palace of marble or flame but a living place, its walls formed by the trunks of ancient trees whose branches interwove high above, their emerald canopy filtering the sun into shifting mosaics of green and gold. Shafts of light lanced through the leaves, catching on drifting motes of pollen and incense smoke that coiled lazily upward like faint spirits.

The eight Diathan were gathered around Astinmah's long wooden table, carved from the heartwood of a fallen elder oak, its surface veined with time and the faint shimmer of divine sigils. The scent of roasted maize and stewed peppers mingled with fresh earth and damp moss, a mingling of hearth and wild that was uniquely hers. Plates of Chantico's beef and bean tortillas and tamales wrapped in steaming corn husks filled the air with warmth and spice, grounding the meeting of gods in the tangible comfort of mortal food.

Quetzalcoatl, the feathered serpent, took a bite of his tamale and pointed at Ananke. "You asked us to come; why?"

Astinmah nibbled delicately on a corn cob, her moss-green hair catching glints of light like wet leaves as she glanced at her sister. The goddess of chains, bonds, and contracts chewed her beef and bean tortilla with measured precision.

Even here, surrounded by kin, her every motion seemed deliberate,as though every gesture were part of some greater, unseen agreement. When she finally spoke, her voice carried a quiet weight that settled over the table like a tightening cord.

"I think an Ancient god was freed from grèim claigeann."

When Skullcap, the prison of the gods, was mentioned, every Diathan exchanged uneasy glances. The air itself seemed to dim, the green-gold light paling as if the forest listened.

"Are you sure?"

Ananke nodded. "As one of the keepers of grèim claigeann, I'm almost certain that one escaped, though I am not sure which one."

The First Dreamer, Mixcoatl, leaned forward, the subtle gleam of starlight flickering behind his dark eyes. His fingers drummed the edge of the table as though tracing constellations only he could see. "Is this what caused the disruption around? What's the name of that place—Eola?"

From across the table, Huitzilopochtli, the guardian of the wheel, narrowed his eyes. His armor shimmered faintly beneath the dappled light, its gold surfaces catching stray embers from Chantico's nearby fire. "You felt it as well?" he asked, his voice low and resonant, directed toward Mixcoatl, who nodded.

The war god folded his hands across his chest and grunted. "Does this have something to do with your Ridere?"

The goddess nodded, meeting Huitzilopochtli's gaze. "Yes, My Balgair was there. I lost contact with him for a while." Her lips curled in a wistful smile. "He was worried about me."

A faint crackle came from the hearth. Somewhere outside, a breeze stirred the canopy, and the murmur of distant leaves sounded almost like whispered prayers. The tension among the gods eased—if only slightly.

The Feathered Serpent shared a look with the Hearth Mistress, who shrugged. "Will this be a boon or a bane?" he inquired, looking to the goddess in the smoke. "Speak, Despoina, give us your wisdom."

The Akkadian goddess inhaled deeply, her breath drawing in a curl of fragrant smoke from the incense bowl before her. The air around her shimmered with heat and shadow, the smoke winding upward to form transient shapes—faces, wings, fragments of futures that dissolved before meaning could settle. Her eyes drifted closed as she tried to ride the waves of time.

"I can't tell," she admitted, exhaling softly, the smoke wreathing her head like a shifting crown. "Whichever one escaped is at least a minor Diathan." She shook her head, her long dark hair rippling with the movement. "Trying to read him is like trying to read Mac Draoidheachd." She blinked and reached out for one of Chantico's delicious tamales. "I'm sorry I can't be more specific."

"It's okay, sister," Astinmah said with a tender smile. A soft green glow pulsed briefly beneath her skin, a sign of her divine composure returning to the room. "I have faith that if the escapee were malicious, He Who Watches would have warned us." As a nurturing goddess, she had faith in her father, even if the other Diathan were not so sure. "Have you notified your Taghta to keep an eye out for visitors?"

Each of the Diathan nodded. It had been the first thing they had done.

The green-eyed goddess of the forest waved her hand across the table. The branches above stirred at her gesture, scattering soft petals and golden dust across the food and faces of her kin. "Until we learn more, let us not worry too much." She smiled. "Besides, Sister Chantico's food is getting cold."

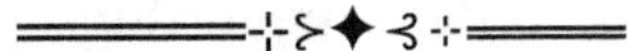

While the Diathan feasted on the Hearth Mistress's fine cuisine, the ancient god sat in shadow, playing idly with the half-cooked ham and egg sandwich that passed for the travelers' breakfast. The cavern around them was dim and airless, lit only by the faint glow of a dying campfire. Smoke curled sluggishly toward a fissure high in the rock, leaving behind the acrid tang of burnt grease and damp stone.

461

Finally, with an unseen look of disgust, he pushed the food away. "Is this the best you can do?"

The two archers, seated a cautious distance from him, likewise pushed their food aside. The faint scrape of tin plates echoed down the cavern tunnel. If they had anything to say about it, there would be food on the wing for lunch or dinner. They longed for open air, for the smell of feathers and pine sap instead of sulfur and cold ash.

Brigid, who had already shoved her food away so she would not throw up, sat curled against the cavern wall. Her breath came in shallow waves. She pressed one hand to her stomach, where the faint warmth of the godling pulsed beneath her palm like a second heartbeat.

The nausea rolled through her again, a reminder of the life, or curse, she carried.

She wondered how long it would take her to start showing, and whether she would survive to see it.

"We didn't expect to have to leave our supplies behind," the assassin commented, taking a bite of the badly cooked food. His voice carried easily in the stillness; even the fire seemed to pause, its embers popping faintly in the silence that followed.

The ancient god's eyes flickered from beneath his hood as he turned toward the assassin. A low hum, like distant thunder, rippled through the air, not sound, but presence. "Would you rather have stayed and fought the invaders?"

He didn't sound angry. He sounded curious, as though testing the shape of the man's will.

The assassin nodded once. "Yes, we could have beaten them or at least diverted them away from you." His right hand dropped to rest on the hilt of his dagger. The firelight gleamed along the blade's edge, a spark of mortal defiance. "The mercenary was after the woman we kidnapped."

The ancient god regarded him for a long moment, the folds of his cowl shifting like liquid shadow. "Could you have defeated them and, after them, the town guard?" His tone remained smooth, not mockery, but genuine inquiry, as if he were studying an experiment in progress.

The assassin pushed away from the wall, letting the food fall to the ground. It landed with a dull slap against the stone.

He paced to the end of the cavern and back again, boots grinding over grit and broken shale. "I think we could have beaten the mercenary and his rescuers." He faced the ancient god squarely now, both hands resting on the hilts of his daggers. "We spent four years building the guilds that ran that building. We spent two more years changing the building to match our needs." His voice hardened. "We left without even fighting for it, and that bothers me."

"Yes, I can see that it would." The ancient god replied smoothly. The cowl tilted slightly to one side, a gesture almost human, though there was nothing human in the power that bled from him.

The fire dimmed for a heartbeat, shadows deepening across the assassin's face.

"Pledge your allegiance to me, assassin, and I'll make sure we go back to your guilds."

Yarsmith's expression froze into something cold and deliberate. He met the god's gaze without flinching. "You have always had my allegiance, great one. Every kill I have made has been dedicated to you." His voice was steady, his body still as stone while the god approached.

"I know," the ancient god replied calmly. "Even locked away in Skullcap, I felt every soul you sent my way. They've fed my pets."

The air thickened as their gazes met,, the faint crackle of embers, the echo of dripping water, the almost inaudible rasp of Brigid's breath. The assassin's anger burned bright and sharp, like a brand in the darkness.

The god's lips curved into a slow, knowing sneer, and the faintest scent of iron rose in the air, as though blood were remembering itself.

He started making plans that included Yarsmith's unique skills. Such was the way of chaos.

After leaving Astinmah's table, Ananke returned to her home plane, a realm of still air and polished marble where golden light pooled in quiet corners.

The silence there was complete, the kind that only gods could hear. She crossed the smooth floor to her wardrobe, the faint echo of her steps swallowed by the heavy hush.

With a sigh that rippled faintly through the air like the settling of chains, she opened the wardrobe doors. Within hung garments of divine make: cloaks of starlight, robes woven from fate-thread, mantles of silk and ash. Her fingers lingered briefly before she selected a green and brown patterned cloak, the colors of the living world, and cast it across her shoulders.

From deeper within, she drew forth a thin-bladed sword whose edge shimmered like liquid moonlight, and a bundle of delicate chains of gold and silver that chimed softly as she gathered them.

They sounded like the echo of vows once spoken.

Praying softly to He Who Watches, Ananke reached upward. The air rippled, and a set of ornate keys shimmered into being, suspended in the ether, each key carved with sigils that pulsed faintly with their own awareness. She clipped them to her belt and turned slowly, her eyes sweeping across her home one last time, the ordered books, the quiet glow of the lamps, the familiar peace of duty delayed too long.

Then she stepped through a pair of Corinthian columns whose stone veined with divine gold, and the light of her realm folded away.

Beyond them lay a desolate wasteland.

The ground stretched endlessly beneath a bruised sky, cracked and colorless.

A dry wind moaned over the barren flats, scattering dust like ancient ash. The scent of ozone and cold iron lingered in the air.

Ananke drew her hood tighter as she gazed at the fifty-foot-high, twenty-foot-thick granite walls that ringed the horizon, the perimeter of Skullcap, the prison of the gods. The granite shimmered faintly, runes etched into its surface glinting with a dull crimson light. Somewhere deep within, she could hear the slow grind of gears, the breath of the prison itself.

It had been millennia since she had last walked this cursed ground, and guilt prickled beneath her calm façade. She had failed in her duty as Mistress of Chains.

Now, she meant to atone.

Determined to uncover which of the Ancients had escaped, Ananke strode toward the massive iron gate. "Greim Claigeann, I, Ananke, Mistress of Chains, seek entrance," she declared, her voice carrying across the wind. The keys at her side jingled in acknowledgment as she raised them toward the barrier.

A ray of dark energy lanced from the gate, scanning her from head to foot, its chill brushing her skin like cold smoke. The light paused upon the keys, then withdrew.

"You may enter, Mistress of Chains, as can your companion," a metallic voice intoned.

"What companion?" Ananke turned sharply, and froze as a shadow detached itself from the jagged rocks behind her.

The figure was slight and graceful, the shape unmistakably feminine. Leather armor caught the faint gleam of starlight as the newcomer stepped forward and pulled back her hood.

"Des? What are you doing here?"

Despoina flashed her a grin that was half mischief, half resignation. "The same thing you are," she said, touching the set of keys at her own belt. She looked up at the towering walls. "I haven't been to Skullcap in millennia."

Ananke nodded, her expression softening with weary understanding. "This is going to be a big job."

"How many ancient gods are in there?" Despoina asked as they passed beneath the gate's shadow and into the prison grounds. The iron bars slid open with a low, mournful groan.

"Nobody knows for sure," Ananke replied, her voice echoing faintly off the black stone. "We have been locking up our own kind for millennia upon millennia, and we wonder why our worshippers are sometimes crazy."

Despoina's gaze swept across the courtyard where spectral sentinels drifted like pale fireflies. "Cerebri, Hecatoncheiri, Nidhogg, Sphinx, Gorgon. I had forgotten who we put in charge of this prison," she murmured as they entered the main building.

They halted as a shadow stirred before them.

"Mistresses."

The sphinx stepped into view, a majestic creature with the body of a lioness, the torso of a woman, and the wings of an eagle dusted in motes of golden light. Her voice reverberated like a chord struck in a vast chamber. "I am Warden Gliocas. How may I help you?" She bowed her head respectfully when she saw the keys each goddess wore, though her golden eyes flicked warily toward the blades at their sides. "And you came armed as well," she noted.

Ananke inclined her head in return. "We have come to check on your prisoners. It's been far too long since we've visited."

The sphinx arched a brow, her feathers ruffling. "I fear that you aren't giving me the full truth."

The faint rustle of Ananke's golden chains filled the air. At once, Gliocas blanched, lowering her gaze. "Forgive me, my impertinence, lady of chains."

Ananke shared a look with Despoina, who shrugged lightly. "We have come to check up on the prisoners, to catalog any new deaths or escapes."

Gliocas froze, her feline tail flicking nervously. "There are no escapes from Greim Claigeann. If any gods have been released, they've been released within the laws of the divine."

Despoina's brow arched. "Have any gods been released lately?" Her fingers brushed the hilt of her thorn blade, the motion casual but unmistakable.

The warden's composure faltered. "To the best of my knowledge, there have been no escapes or releases." She swallowed hard, lowering her head. "Only bearers of chains and scales may have access to the records."

"You are correct," Ananke said calmly. "Have any other chains or scales been here lately?"

Gliocas shook her head. "No, Mistress, you and Mistress Despoina are the first to visit in a millennium. If any have escaped, I will bear full responsibility."

"That won't be necessary," Despoina said gently, the smoke around her seeming to soften the edges of her form. "I don't believe there has been an escape. If any are gone, they've regained their freedom using the old ways."

Ananke nodded solemnly.

The warden blinked, comprehension dawning, and fear. "That would mean that they found new worshippers and gained enough spiritual power to get out," she murmured. "That rarely happens."

The Mistress of Chains exhaled slowly, the sound like the clink of distant links. "Where is the records office? If any got released, the orbs will record the time and date and which priestess woke them."

Gliocas extended one wing toward a corridor lined with torchlight. "The Akashic records are kept there."

Despoina was already striding forward, the hem of her cloak stirring the dust. "Come along, Warden. We have many records to search and have to see who has been released."

"Yes, Mistress," Gliocas replied, falling in step behind them, her claws clicking softly against the marble floor.

The hall opened into a vast chamber filled with a faint hum, as though the air itself remembered every voice that had ever spoken within.

"Welcome to the Akashic records of Greim Claigeann. How may I help you, Mistress Ananke and Mistress Despoina?"

The goddesses looked around, and saw two different worlds.

To Ananke, the chamber appeared as a library of scrolls, each resting in a cubby carved from white stone, the air perfumed faintly with dust and ink.

To Despoina, it was a living sea of smoke, undulating like thought itself, the shapes within shifting with every flicker of her imagination.

"How many gods reside here, imprisoned?" Ananke asked.

"There are over five hundred greater powers, a thousand lesser powers, and fifty demi-powers," replied the records.

Despoina extended a finger, letting the smoke coil around it like a curious serpent. "How many have passed through the veils and into the outer darkness?"

"Since the last visit by a scale, fifty greater powers have passed on, as have a hundred lesser powers, and five demi-powers have ceased to exist."

Despoina blinked, the smoke dimming around her hand. "That is quite a lot. It means whole faiths have been expunged from existence." A shiver passed through her voice. "I cannot imagine how it feels to have every follower suddenly stop believing in you."

"Indeed," Ananke murmured, eyes on the glowing scrolls before her. The silence pressed close. "How many have met the requirements for release?"

The chamber brightened as the Akashic records answered immediately:

"Since the last visit by a chain, only one god has been released."

"I wonder who," Ananke whispered.

"The trickster god, Iktomi."

The air shifted. Light gathered to form an image, a great spider woven from shadow and firelight, its many eyes glimmering with intelligence and mischief.

Ananke frowned, studying the glowing records. "Why was Iktomi imprisoned? If memory serves, he wasn't an evil god. He didn't cause any widespread destruction, nor did he instigate a rebellion against He Who Watches."

Despoina leaned closer, her eyes narrowing at a gap in the text. "Can you tell us who imprisoned him and what for?"

A pause, then the voice of the records spoke again:

"Iktomi, the spider god, was brought in and turned over by his brother Inyan for being a Chaotic disruptor."

"That's no reason for imprisonment," Ananke said softly. "It's not like he destroyed anything."

"How long was he imprisoned?" Despoina asked, her tone hushed.

"The records show that he has been imprisoned for almost two millennia. Whope judged him, and Wakan Tanka locked him up."

Despoina sighed, her breath scattering the smoke into delicate spirals. "Exactly when did Iktomi meet the requirements for release, and who is the priestess who gained him his release?"

The records pulsed once, accessing the past.

"The records show that a priestess by the name of Brigid Arisdottir petitioned for his release. Her claims were validated, and he was released."

For a long moment, neither goddess spoke. The faint hum of divine memory filled the silence.

Then Ananke bowed her head. "Thank you, Archive." Without waiting for a response, she turned and began walking back toward the corridor, her cloak whispering against the floor.

When Despoina joined her, the two sisters exchanged a solemn look.

"We must tell Astinmah and the rest that Iktomi is free in our world," Despoina said quietly, her voice carrying the weight of foreknowledge. "And that he might not be mentally stable."

Their footsteps echoed through the long stone hall, a sound that faded, but did not end.

Let's Keep in Touch (and in Tales)

I hope you enjoyed reading this book as much as I did writing it.

If you wish to read other books I've written, you will find them, in order, below.

The Draoidh's Cearcall (Series)

1—The Draoidh's Cearcall

Forthcoming

2 — The Draoidh's Gambit

3 — The Shadows Rise

The Law Keeper Chronicles (Series)

1 — The Black Swan's Bond

Forthcoming

2 — The Sheriff's Oath

3 — By Law and Flame

The Web-Weaver's War (Series)

Forthcoming

1 — Oath & Ember

If you want to tag along for the fun, join my mailing list at:

https://josephwiess.substack.com/